A LIFE FORGED IN DEATH

TANYA DECLERCQ

WEBSITE

www.GeminiAuthor.com

A Life Forged In Death

This is a work of fiction. Any similarities to any people, past or present, are purely coincidental, and would be very surprising to the author. The characters, and what they endure, are from the imagination of the author. Any places, people, or time periods referenced that may exist are not used as a reality, but fictitiously to build the story. An indie author wrote and published this book, so basically please do not steal my hard work, or that of those I hired, so I can continue to make my dream come true.

To follow/support the author, please check out her webpage at:
www.GeminiAuthor.com

There you will find a blog, newsletter for updates and exclusive opportunities, a chat option, contact form, links to all her social media accounts, as well as her published work.

Editor: Chandi Broadbent & Kristina Parker
Cover Art: Gemini Moon Publishing, LLC
Formatting: Ravenswood Publishing & Goods
ravenswoodpg@gmail.com

ISBN (Paperback - Color): 979-8-218-16804-9
ISBN (Paperback – Black & White):979-8-218-12026-9

TRIGGER WARNINGS:

Adult themes
Non/Dub Con
Reimagined historical elements
Death
Mild sexual content

ACKNOWLEDGMENTS

We all live with dreams, or what ifs, in our lives. I was terrified. Honestly, I still am, about writing this book. To put myself out there takes away the what if and places it firmly in the "it's happened" category. I now hope that both my sons, Nicolas and Christopher, see this and always remember to chase their dreams, today and every day. They are the reason I get up each morning. I love them both, more than they will ever truly know. Without them, and the support of others, this would have likely remained a what if forever.

To my best friend, Ashley aka crAshley, (you know I had to), you have helped me find my way with this book and in life. I will always remember to keep pushing forward. To my best friend Christine, your reminder on so many mornings that there are more what ifs left to conquer has been a reminder that we cannot live without trying. I may never make it to Hollywood, but I can dream. To my beta readers, ARC team, and everyone who has supported me in any way, I sincerely appreciate each and every one of you. Oh, and those that know me personally, yes, I've always been this weird, but just wait till book two... it gets worse. So much worse.

CHAPTER 1
~ JENNA ~

If you are looking for a love story, you are going to be sorely disappointed. This is simply my tale, my life, as it has come to pass over the years. I was raised well, with a family that loved me, only wished the best for me. The only child, I admit now, I wanted for nothing. My father was a prominent solicitor while Mother embodied all that elite society considered proper. A standard she instilled in me from birth. They had planned to arrange the perfect marriage for me, one that would improve my position.

They held secrets, though, that I could never imagine.

But I get ahead of myself. Let me start the night everything changed. The night my happiness suffered the first cut, only to be torn apart in the following months. As you read my story, keep but one thought in mind: To survive is to adapt.

. . .

The day was glorious. One filled with joy, and, I admit, the giggles of a naïve young woman granted a taste of freedom by her parents. A dress of silk and lace that grazed the floor and hugged each curve of my upper body. I had worn nothing more lovely in all my years. The warm peach color contrasted with the pale hue of my skin and mahogany brown locks of hair that curled to frame my face. Staring at my reflection, my chocolate eyes glistened back with happiness threatening to spill forth, only to halt at the call from downstairs.

"Jenna dear, we must make haste." Mother's voice held warning as it raced up the stairs to the open door.

How my heart soared while my feet carried me down the grand spiral staircase to the waiting carriage. Mother insisted upon arriving in a manner befitting our status, despite the short ride. We rode in the finest of the several carriages we kept at the manor. The black canopy catching glimmers of light along the street, which reminded me of the stars beginning to dominate the sky above. Nights made me believe that magic may truly exist.

The ball was the first I was permitted to attend since coming of age. In truth, many women younger than me were already wed. Mother, in surprising fashion, had been hesitant to permit any to call upon us. When my twentieth birthday came, she relented to my father's insistence. I did not mind, as none had succeeded in capturing my attention. That was, until he returned home.

My heart fluttered whenever my eyes were granted the sight of him. If rumors held truth, his heart reciprocated. Tonight, he would make his intentions known by requesting permission to call upon our house.

Trent Rathborne came from a very respected family. His father served within an official capacity in the courts, and ran the largest firm dealing with financial matters, which to me, were a bore. His mother was known for holding the most prestigious tea parties for the women of the elite. He was the perfect match for my parents' intentions.

My life would be splendidly divine. I could see the house I would call my home, the children who would play at my feet, the man I would lie beside each night. I saw the world through rose-colored glasses. Evil did not exist. The only darkness was the night. Even that was never all consuming, with the moon casting its glow across the sky. Trent and I would be lucky enough to have our happily ever after.

The event was magical. Lord and Lady Rathborne always threw the most lavish affairs, which all invited attended and others read about in the morning edition. Music carried each couple around the floor, their eyes locked in a subtle conversation none would speak aloud in polite society. Perhaps that was what I simply wished to think as I stood beside my parents. Blue and silver tablecloths reflected glimmers of the ensconced light on the walls. Pearl white curtains encased the windows, enhancing the beauty of the room with hints of the moonlight just beyond.

Atop the tables, the finest foods were set out to satisfy the meager appetites of the guests. None would indulge too much, for fear of becoming a meal for the wagging tongues of gossips. Women wore their finest gowns with jewels gracing every neckline, daring men's eyes to linger. Men wore tailored suits, ties or ascots firmly in place with cuff links displayed on each wrist.

A waltz carried each couple across the dance floor. Silent nods exchanged with those observing in satisfaction of being seen. Everything was about perception. A gilded cage we thrived in willingly.

"Good evening, Mr. and Mrs. Devereaux. We are pleased you could attend." Lord Rathborne spoke above the melody.

"It is our honor." Father gave a small nod before both men laughed.

"My wife wished to celebrate Trent's homecoming properly, where I had wished him to simply begin working."

"We never do win those battles."

"No, we do not, Edmund." Lord Rathborne's use of my father's name was not shocking, as they had been friends for years. Another reason I knew they would approve of our affections for one another.

Trent cleared his throat beside his mother, his hand stretching out in offering. "May I have this dance?"

I saw the grins spread along our fathers' faces, the imperceptible look of permission from my own. I fought to hold back my excitement as I slid my white gloved hand in his.

He escorted me to the floor in time for a new melody to begin. The gleam in his eye spoke of his intent. Other men were to take note that he had staked his claim. All was right within my world. Each song brought us closer into each other's embrace until he whisked me away to the balcony. Certain none noticed us escape through a set of French doors, we turned to face each other.

His suit did little to hide the tall, muscular frame beneath, which I often dreamt of. A blush took residence along my cheeks as thoughts of innocence lost snuck their way in. Standing under the moonlight, his deep caramel eyes held mine, a wisp of his sandy colored hair falling across his forehead. He was the most handsome man I had ever seen.

I wished to stop time; stay as we were forever. Holding each other too close for propriety's sake, he pulled me closer still, to barely brush his lips against mine. My eyes closed to welcome my first kiss.

"Excuse me, young man, but I believe the lady does not belong to you. You would do well to rejoin the festivities." His deep voice had an edge that caused the hairs upon the back of my neck to stand on end. He stood there, his manner of dress a slight contrast to others in attendance. Though the black suit cut perfectly into his figure, he wore a blood red shirt beneath, without a tie or ascot. His ebony hair accompanied almost black eyes that were set off against olive skin, the combination making him remarkably handsome. Embarrassment over being caught in such an act, by what I could only assume was a regal guest, caused my cheeks to flush, even as Trent began to pull me back inside.

Passing the stranger, I was startled when he reached out to halt our progress, his hand clasped around my arm. "You smell heavenly, my lady. I wish to enjoy your company further. We shall dance to the next song."

"You will unhand her, sir..." Trent's voice shook with outrage, only to trail off when he met the stranger's eyes. Time seemed to stop. My heart hammered within my chest, my eyes begged Trent to continue. To my dismay, he but nodded before making his way back toward the other young men crowded in a far corner of the room. I stood there looking after him, dumbfounded. I did not even realize I had moved until I felt the stranger place one hand upon my waist whilst he lifted my left hand in the other.

A slow melody rose into the air, familiar yet too distant for my ears to clearly hear. My eyes refused to part from the man across from me as all else faded into the background. A flurry of life surrounded us, yet did not exist. I was a puppet on a string that he held tightly within his grasp. A strange sensation moved me, compelled me to do what he wished without a single word uttered. I do not know how many songs I spent in his arms before he guided me from the dance floor to my parents. They eyed him with a suspicion that did little to give him pause.

In a moment, he leaned down and whispered in my ear, his words sending a chill down my spine, "You smell delicious. Soon, I will savor the taste of you on my lips."

Fear shattering the fog, I turned to face him. He was gone. Only the crowded room met me while I sought him out. Unnerved, I felt suddenly ill. Mother looked momentarily dazed;

her head shook as I had seen her do only once before, when she had gotten too far into father's liquor cabinet. Tonight, not a single drop had passed her lips. Father simply wore a nervous expression, then drank his glass of bourbon in a single swallow.

"Father. Mother. I am not well. Might we leave?"

"We cannot leave yet, dear. It would not be seemly." Mother wore a concerned expression as she struggled between her love for me and the imagined stain that would befall our reputation.

"Perhaps go splash some cold water on your face, Jenna. I am sure you will be fine." Father did not even spare me a glance. The young servant with a tray of drinks was his sole focus for the moment.

"Please, I beg of you. I must leave this place. I need to go home." Despite my attempts, my voice rose in desperation.

The few nearby glanced our way, which made me straighten my spine. No matter my mother's teachings, I always felt a little suffocated by the rules.

If only her next words had been different. If she had not acquiesced, my fate may not have been sealed.

"Take the carriage. See that you return home straight away, then send the carriage back for us. I had informed the staff that we would be late so they will not be up to attend you."

"I will head straight to bed." I felt relieved that I was granted permission, placed a quick kiss to her cheek before gathering my skirt and making my way toward the front entrance.

Trent stepped in front of me, blocking my path just as I was about to cross the threshold. "Where are you off to? You promised me the final dance."

"A dance?" My voice rose, causing me to take a few breaths to calm myself before continuing. "We have danced our dances, Sir. All before you left me to that... that man. Now, I wish to return home. If you still desire to call upon me, you shall need to speak with my parents." Rushing around him before tears spilled forth, I made my way to our carriage.

"Miss?" Johnathon stood by some of the others that waited for their employers to leave.

"I am not well. I need to get home, then you can return for my parents." The words rushed out; my expression, I thought, must look even worse given the way he hastened to take the reins.

With each step the horses took, the night played through my mind. The glow of admiration that I held for Trent had begun to show signs of tarnish. How could he have let that man step in? Why did he not return to intervene? The event that was supposed to be a pivotal moment in my life paled greatly under the shadow of a stranger. A stranger that made me question the state of my mind.

So consumed, I absentmindedly waved Johnathon off to return for my parents while I made my way up the stairs to the solid double doors. Home. The sight lifted the weight oppressing me a fraction of the way. I felt eyes on me with every step. Reaching the sanctity of my room, I shut the door hard, my back pressed against the wood as I took several slow, deep breaths. I could not shake the sensation that I was not alone.

I began to search everywhere. Dropping to my knees, I lifted the bed skirt to look under my bed for the monster waiting to grasp my ankles on approach. I flung open the door to my private bath, then moved to check my wardrobe. Gone was the pretense of shedding the last of my childhood for the woman I had become. I was a woman in body, led by a child's irrational mind that was questioning every creak, feared every shadow. I stood in the center of the room, eyes searching for what, I was not sure.

The man was odd. Fact. You were extremely excited for what tonight meant. Fact. Trent had told you before, once he graduated, he would then think of his future. Fact. A woman can be prone to hysterics and her mind will create misconceptions. Fact, according to father, anyway. I could not stop the small scoff at the thought. That defiance lessening the tension.

"Was he right? Was I so lost to what I dreamt of that one minor disruption sent my thoughts into a frenzy of nonsense? We danced, yet the entire world kept going in and out of focus around us. Even now, I cannot clear the image of the time I spent with… I don't even know the man's name!" I moved to pace but found myself still glancing about, as if I expected the stranger to appear.

"How many times had I told father he was wrong about women? Are we really so easily thrown into fits of insanity? I will not allow it. I am sane. I am a woman, and I am sane." I let out a long, slow breath.

Realizing the folly of my actions, I let loose a laugh that sounded even to my ears a mix of madness and ease. To prove myself the woman I wished to be, I walked boldly to the French doors leading to my balcony on the second floor and opened them wide, welcoming the night air. This was my proof I could over-come immature hysterics. Standing in the open, I closed my eyes, took a few deep breaths to erase the last coils of tension that held residence within my body.

The moonlight danced along my beautiful peach dress, a sight that once more brought a small smile to my lips. I traced my hands down the gown while I moved back inside. In a joyous display, I twirled round and round within my chambers, arms outstretched, with my head positioned toward the ceiling.

Faster I spun, the action caused the skirt to float away from my body. True happiness filled my heart at the promise of tomor-row. A new day would bring a chance for new possibilities. The stranger had never been seen before, therefore likely never would be seen again. Silently, I admonished myself for acting like a silly girl. I was a woman now, ready to court, to marry. Ready for my new life to unfold. Beginning to feel dizzy, the room spun of its own volition, but still I pushed, promising myself this was the last night of whimsy I would allow.

Ready to collapse, I surrendered to gravity, my body given permission to fall to a heap on the floor. Only the floor did not meet me. Swept up from my descent, the soft contour of my mattress replaced where the hard floor should have been. A heaviness lay at my side, warm breath caressed my cheek.

"So delicious. So intoxicating. What do you hide in your blood, little one?" That voice, deep and ominous, sealed my breath in my lungs. My eyes shot open to dispel what I hoped was a nightmare. A figment of imagination from hitting my head on the floor. Only the crème-colored ceiling was absent. Two dark eyes filled my vision, slowly morphing into pools of crimson.

My voice found at last, I screamed in terror. He quickly covered my mouth, a laugh filtering from his own that revealed what I swore were large sharp teeth. Moving to leave his side, his hand pressed firmly into my abdomen to keep me in place. I squirmed, but it was a futile attempt that brought only amusement to his eyes. Red eyes that wickedly surveyed my body. He moved his hand to push strands of hair off my face.

"Please. Please leave me. I beg of you to show mercy." The tears I had held back released in a wave to stream down the sides of my face into my hair.

"Do not fret, little one. It will only hurt briefly. Then all will fade into nothing. Though maybe not. You are a delight, so perhaps if you are a really good girl, I will give you some of my blood. Might be interesting to see what happens." He laughed as he spoke. His last word ushering forth while he moved to lay further across my body. Fear of what was to come had many outcomes, but none prepared me for the sudden pain I felt sear my neck. He pushed me further up my pillow, my head lifted, my neck stretched more in unwelcomed invitation.

Something dripped a path down my chest, warm and slick

with a faint coppery aroma. He had told the truth. My struggles eased. The intrusion of fangs piercing my flesh faded. A haze more intense than before consumed me. Staring up into oblivion, there was only the heat of his body pressing down, the feel of his lips on my skin, his hands trailing down my body over my gown, ready to subdue without cause, for I could no longer rebel.

A feeling of pleasure, of peace, filled the void of pain and fear left in their wake. There on top of the taupe-colored bed, I felt myself detach, impossibly looking down at the scene below. The room faded into darkness until it became nothing.

That was the night I died. The night Jenna Devereaux truly ceased to exist.

"This cannot be real." My words held little conviction, slipping out between parted lips in a whispered prayer that received no reply.

A tremble began in my fingers, traveled up my arms, then spread throughout my body. My eyes were open, but I could not see anything. Musty air filled my lungs with every quick breath. Beneath my feet lay cold stone. The floor was damp dirt which squished between my toes with every step I took. My hands held out in front of me, I attempted to find the wall without running into it.

My fingers splayed against the wall, a discovery that gave me a small reprieve from the solid lump of fear in my throat. Remembering, my hand sought to feel for evidence of the bite I was certain I had suffered. I only felt smooth skin being dirtied by whatever coated my fingers. Hope rose to combat the despair, my voice rough when it found its way out.

"Hello? Is anyone there? I need help! Hello? Someone? Anyone? Father?" I sidestepped along the wall until I found what I assumed to be the door. My small hands fisted to pound against it while I called out.

A creak sounded, followed by the scratching noise of a latch. The door swung inward, sending me back several steps. Relief filled me with the glow of light until I saw my would-be savior.

"My, my, you are full of surprises. I had hoped you would not pass, but I did not think you would actually survive after my little feast. Most assuredly you would not possess the strength to rise."

"What have you done to me? My father will pay you for my release. Let me go, please." I tried to sound brave, but the cracks in my voice told the truth.

He stood there without a word. Gone was his suit, clad in loose black pants without a shirt. I could see the muscles in his chest twitch. He set the lantern on a small shelf on the wall, then turned to lock the door with a key he slipped back into his pocket. When he took a step toward me, I knew I was not going home. That knowledge opened the floodgate. My vision blurred behind the salty downpour, my head shaking as I murmured over and over.

"I do not want to die."

"Shhhh." He grabbed me by the arms and pushed me back towards the bed. "Everyone dies eventually, my tasty morsel."

He made me lay down, all fight within me lost. He would bite me again and this time I would not survive. I welcomed the end. My only regret that my parents might never know what became of me. I closed my eyes, the hot tears rolling down my cheeks. Only, he did not bite my neck. I felt him shift his weight a second before I felt his large hands grip my dress to tear it from my body.

My eyes sprung open with renewed panic. I grabbed at the fabric to cover myself, but when I turned to claw at his face, he wrapped both wrists in one of his hands. Arms stretched above my head, he lowered his face to mine, his other hand on my chin to keep my gaze on his. He appeared happy. A smile caressed his lips; his eyes devoured all they could feast on.

"Fight me. I like it when you do. Makes your blood so much more potent." With each word, he lowered himself on top of me, then rocked his hips to confirm his intentions.

"No. Do not do this. Kill me if you must, but please..." Words failed me when his hand dropped from my chin to pinch my nipple between his fingers.

"Go ahead. Keep begging." He drove his hips forward harder, and I felt the length confined within his pants.

He wanted me to beg, to cry, to fall apart. Inside something snapped. My tears dried, my breath became even, but my eyes held fast to my hatred. I was determined to not give him what he wanted when he was set on taking what I could not stop.

"Quiet now, huh? I will have you screaming by the time I am through with you."

I struggled to free my hands as he took to binding them to the bed frame. It was a waste of energy. I was no match for him. Every blow I landed had no effect. I succeeded in a slap to his face, my nails rewarded in thin bloody streaks that dried almost instantly. My breath became erratic as I tried to make sense of what was happening. There was no time. As soon as my hands were secure, he tore the last fragments of my clothing away.

My momentary resolve shattered under the realization of what was to come. He stood beside the bed, his hands undid his pants, allowing them to drop to the floor. I saw the eagerness of his desire spring forth to erase all doubt. He crawled onto the bed; my legs kicked to discourage him, but that only earned me a hard slap across my cheek. My vision blurred, ears ringing as pain lanced through my skull.

Every dream I had of tenderness vanished. His rough palms groped every inch of my body. His teeth nipped at the sensitive flesh of my neck. These were not the playful taunts of a lover; he was reminding me of what he had already done and planned to do again. I was helpless beneath him, the strength I tried to project a charade betrayed by the soft sobs I could not stop.

Pleased with himself, I could feel a sickening wetness on my abdomen, his right hand gripping my hip in a brutal hold. He bit down. Not the savagery of before, but more than enough to release the current hidden within my veins. He sucked slowly, savoring the taste of my blood as men enjoyed their bourbon. The glimmer that this would be all faded when the first digit broke the barrier of my core.

A fresh wave of tears unleashed with a scream that only increased his thrusts. One finger became two. Two became three. The palm of his hand added pressure to the sensitive bundle of nerves. My body responded, void of the hatred, shame, and guilt I felt in every muscle.

"Give in to me." His voice was strained. Blood coated his lips when he raised his head to stare down at me.

He kissed me hard, his hand never slowing the rhythm of his fingers deep inside my body. I wanted to bite off the tongue that pushed past my lips, but I knew that would somehow make things much worse for me. Still, I could not resist warning him by allowing my teeth to graze the intrusive object. I tasted metal, but the act only sent him into a frenzy. His fingers claimed my body until the traitorous thing convulsed around him. I felt weak, spent, yet on fire. The tension that coiled deep within unwound to travel along every nerve at once. Trying to close my legs, they shook, though they held no weight. Despite the sensation, I gagged as hot tears fell from my eyes.

He raised his hand to his mouth, eyes on mine as each finger was licked clean. I did not have time to think of what he had done, as his hands grabbed to pull my thighs further apart, his body sliding down only to piston back up. His manhood slammed into the tight channel of my body that stretched to accommodate him.

He stilled, knowing this hurt more than my body, and he wanted to prolong the moment.

His hips circled, drawing back an inch, only to slam forward. I shut my eyes, trying to send my mind anywhere but here. Another slap brought me back to the horrific reality. His lips sucked and bit my breasts, hands roamed freely as he drove deep in a hungry rhythm. I lost count of how many times he made me orgasm. For hours he used my body for his enjoyment. He fed on my blood and when I resisted finding any pleasure in him; he forced me to feed on his.

Biting his lip countless times, he then kissed me to make certain I drank some before he healed. Under the influence of his blood, I was lost within my body. I succumbed to the lust, welcomed the way the dark red fluid washed away thought and feeling. A switch deep inside turned off each time, and I began to plead for it. I did not want to be here, be with this monster that took everything of who I am away from me.

I lost track of time. There were only meager meals followed by long sessions with him. I had learned his name was Victor only when he demanded I call out as I came. The only reprieve was his blood, which I craved to take me away. I was insatiable, needing the next drop as much as I needed air to fill my lungs. My solitary escape from this torment rested within my tormentor.

Madness or death, both may as well be the same fate.

CHAPTER 3
~ JENNA ~

"I will not allow it! This is our daughter, Edmund. She will stay here with us no matter how long it takes. She was gone, Edmund. Two weeks. I thought I had lost my daughter for two weeks. Two horrific weeks that I had to endure under the weight that I was to blame for her disappearance. If I had not permitted her to leave, then...." Gertrude shivered despite the warmth of the fire two meters from them.

"Do you think this is my wish, Gertrude? We cannot help her. The physicians cannot help her. Many speak of her dancing with that strange man and have already spread rumors that she is ill because she is with child. Especially after her vanishing. Then she reappears in her bed, dirty, wearing a scrap of fabric with bloody stains down her body. The physician confirmed she was...." His throat forbid more words from forming.

I lay in my bed, my eyes refused to open. Each time they tried, the light of the room assaulted them as harshly as the midday sun. My body shook violently, then fell still. A trauma response, I heard the physician call it. Given my appearance, they agreed I had to have been taken, or at least held, against my will. A captive.

Used. Used in every way he desired. The moments when I held enough strength, I told my parents of my ordeal, but I could not bring myself to utter the details. They knew. Mother asked gently and my immediate sobs had her clutching me in her embrace. Father startled us both when he punched the wall of my room. The indentation a new decoration by the door.

Now they argue down the hall. Their voices fading in and out, yet never quiet enough to give me peace. I hate that I am the cause of their suffering, that I cannot bring an end to their torment. I hate that I feel guilt as fully as I feel the blanket that covers me. I had no control, but I feel somehow to blame. He took my choice from me. He took my life from me. Their decision is moot. I accepted days ago that my future was forfeited. If I cannot get vengeance, I can at least give them comfort. They did all they could for me since I was born. I refuse to allow my death to cast a cloud over their remaining days.

"Lord Rathborne has forbidden his son from calling upon her, even if she recovers. Gone for weeks, returned for another week, yet cannot even leave her bed. They are right, we can do no more for her. They can make her comfortable, provide the care she needs, save her soul." Father's voice held defeat in every word, pleaded with her to see reason.

From atop my bed, I listened to their discussion. How long had I been awake this time? I had vague recollections of my mother, father, even the physician who had seen to my care since delivering me, speaking to me through a fog I could not disperse. Trying to wake fully, to urge my mind to think rationally, I focused on my parents' voices in the next room. From the scents and slight rustling, the scene was practically visible to my mind's eye.

Father was decisive, always. I had never known him to waver once a decision was made. Even matters as trivial as his choice of tie color were absolute. I wished to call out to my mother, to beg her not to permit what I knew to be on the path he had chosen. I could hear the skirts of her dress bunching, her tiny feet wearing down the rug before him, then all was silent. Neither moved, neither spoke. An eternity passed to the ticking of the clock before I heard her sit.

"Gerty, my heart, I love her too. She is our life, but there is nothing more we can do for her. She has been racked with tremors, soaked through all bedding we place beneath her within a day's time, and has not been able to eat. The physicians do not even understand how she yet lives. This is no life for her. Not like this. They will make her comfortable. They will see to keeping all matters private. We must salvage what is left of our name, else we risk losing all." His footsteps toward her were slow, but I could hear when my mother at last sobbed into his chest.

There it was. I would be sent off to the convent to die. Discarded in the night to stories of my passing from some illness, no doubt. My clothing and bedding would be burned, to show the family had taken all the necessary precautions. I had witnessed other families perform the same act, both when illness and disgrace had cast shadows on their doorsteps. What was wrong with me? I attempted to do all that I was instructed yet no relief was found.

Only minimal wounds covered my body when I first returned home. My near comatose state gave rise to whispers among the staff that I had sacrificed some animal and drenched myself in its blood, was part of a spell that had gone wrong. Now, I was left to pay the price for some unspeakable act. The dress and bedding that bore the evidence were no more. They had found the blood on my bed in my absence, but they had decided to burn that in the fireplace of my room as well, after they had alerted the authorities.

When the search parties found no trace of me, father had burned it in a fit of rage. I heard mother say something about it during a moment of lucidity. The bedspread had provided no clues, simply evidence that I had come to harm. A fact he refused to face.

The dress I hoped would usher in the next stage of my life, had instead stolen my life from me. I had not been the perfect daughter, but I had been good. The whispers on the tongues of the elite never raised a doubt as to our honor. I attempted countless times, when I was able to remain awake, to discern what act earned such a fate as this.

Mother once more came to my side, a cool rag in her hands to place on my forehead. A kiss to my cheek before she lay beside me, lightly stroking my hand told me she had come to deliver their decision. I forced my eyes open, wincing at the blinding light and pain the small gesture caused. I schooled my face, turning to her as I placed my other hand over hers and tried to sound brave.

"It is ok, mother. I know, and I am ready. I love you and father dearly. Do not blame him for what must be done. When will I leave?" Fighting against the hot tears leaving my eyes was of little use. They made their path down into my hair to mix with the perspiration that saturated every strand. I did not wish to go, but I could not bear to cause them more grief.

My mother would not look from our fingers, interlocking them and squeezing them tightly. Her voice was so frail, so small, that I wondered as to how it escaped her lips. "Tonight."

Overwhelmed with emotion, she abruptly sat up to run from the room. Four words spoken through sobs, muffled by hands covering her face. "I love you, Jenna."

Then she was gone. I lay there alone, watching the shadows dance along the wall, the light fading just outside the French doors to my balcony. I wondered if she would return, if father would come to say his goodbyes. The shadows moved across the wall, stretching out in an attempt to seal me in their tomb. The convent would be my tomb. I would never set eyes again upon mother or father.

CHAPTER 4
~ JENNA ~

The ride was unpleasant. Every pebble the carriage wheels traversed felt like a boulder that shook the confined space. A black shawl wrapped around me, covering my face to any that may seek to discover the occupant. A letter, crisp with a dark red seal, waited in the driver's breast pocket. I knew my father had paid him handsomely for his discretion on this late-night endeavor. One that would nonetheless slip from drunken lips later. Secrets were never really secrets, no matter the effort.

I cried while curled up on the bolstered seat, however, my thoughts remained at home. Father could not bring himself to face me. Mother could only sob in her room as the physician aided in sending me off. I wanted to hate them, beg them, hurt them, hug them... This had never been my plan. The disgrace. The life cut short.

The nuns waited on me without fail. My eyes opened to daylight or darkness without sense of the time that had passed. Later I would learn only a few more days of the agony I endured had passed. I woke with a thirst that the clay pitcher beside my bed could not quench. The young lady kneeling in prayer beside me hastened her efforts while she watched the water flow down my neck to soak the light nightgown I wore. I do not know what she saw next. I do recall the look on her face. Wide eyes, mouth agape, hope lost. She was frozen in place when I walked to her, knelt in front of her in confusion, and watched as my own hand raised to expose her neck.

I felt power, strength, hunger, life; I did not understand how everything seemed to move so slowly until the taste of a sweet wine tantalized my tongue. Warm, strange, intoxicating. I wanted more. There were so many different tastes, unique aromas that called to me through the stone walls. I was gluttonous for each drop that slid down my throat. I could hear drums echoing off the walls that summoned me to dance, sing and drink.

So, I did. I drank, found each beat of the drums, dancing and humming from here to there until there was only silence.

I sat on the rug that covered the floor of the chapel; a stained-glass window high on the wall lending its color to the moonlight. In my arms, I held a woman who looked twice my age. Her eyes were glassy, her mouth open as if she were trying to speak. Straining, I listened to find a faint rhythm and suddenly realized what I had done. The drums...

"You're a monster."

I lowered her, looked at my hands covered in layers of blood. They did not seem to be mine. I stood slowly, walking out into the night with memories of stories young boys told to young girls in attempts to scare them. Tales of monsters that drank blood, killed girls in the dark of night, but never would you see them during the day. I ran toward a stream I did not know existed.

Chilly water splashed with each step until I sank deep within its depths. I was buried in the current from my shoulders down, water washing the evidence of my sins away. Dipping below the surface, part of me wished to never again permit air to fill my lungs. Perhaps ceasing to exist now would allow me to pass the gates of paradise. The survival instinct was too great to deny. I found myself crawling onto the rocks along the side, unable to differentiate the tears that flowed down my face from the river water that escaped my hair.

An acute pain cut through my despair like a finely sharpened sword through air. Flashes of images from both my recent feast and of things my eyes have never seen crossed my vision. One word pounding in place of my heartbeat.

"Come," a masculine voice beckoned. As swiftly as the pain set upon me, it vanished. The sudden urge to move compelled me to climb from where I lay half in the water.

Rising, my reflection was disfigured in the ripples that fled from me. I did not miss the flash of red, two spots that peered back at me. My tongue slipped over my teeth in fascination of the sharp points found where blunter ends once resided. There was no fear. No longer did I feel the dampness of the thin gown that clung to my body. I felt nothing at all.

In the distance, the highest point of the convent stood above the trees. I could recall each face, each request for mercy, each taste. I knew if I went back, I would find walls splashed with blood, throats ripped open, even my own blood under some of their fingernails. To look at me now, you would find no wound, and the only blood the stain among my clothes.

My nails cut into my palms as I stood tall, hands fisted at my sides. The pain was what I wanted. I wanted to feel, to etch this moment in my memory forever. Somehow, I understood I had died. Who I was ceased to exist that night, and since that fateful encounter, I had been reborn. The monsters from the tales were real, and I was one.

I opened my hands to view the marks I made, proof, however small, that I existed, that perhaps there was hope. The blood was minimal, crescent cuts healing while I observed them. I knelt to wash, hearing my father's voice speak of women and their frailty. How they go mad or become numb. He had been speaking of women locked away in far worse places by their families.

I walked toward the horizon, accepting the shield of being numb to avoid going mad. Every step I took was accompanied by the screams only my ears heard, the horror only my eyes saw, the demand that I feel the weight of what I had done. My existence required death, required blood. I could not say how I knew, but it was as certain to me as the moon in the sky overhead.

"Come."

CHAPTER 5
~ JENNA ~

I walked. My feet, cut by the dirt road, healed before the next step was taken. I did not care if the nightgown I wore was not proper for public display. Were I to be known, the elite would have a season's worth of gossip. My family would never recover from such a scandal, our good name forever ruined, if it were not so already. There was somewhere I had to be. I had to keep going, no matter what.

Passing families working their land or going about their day, most called out to inquire about my well-being. All were too unnerved to approach, apart from one woman who quietly placed a shawl around my shoulders. Habit had me wrapping it with some modesty, while my pace never wavered. I never responded. I never took my eyes from the road ahead.

"Come."

The sun beamed down; the warmth drying the tattered and stained garment I wore. Only when I heard a child whisper his shock about the state of my dress had I paused. That moment lent opportunity for another revelation. I squinted up toward the glowing orb, with thoughts that I should be ablaze. If I was the monster from the tales, I should have burnt to ash when the rays first touched my skin. I had instead walked through more than half the day facing the sun.

That contradiction broke me. I ran where I saw clothes hung out to dry, acquired what was needed, and broke free of the desire to maintain my course. As I moved, I swore the air attempted to turn me. The ground gave way under my feet. Everything within nature came alive to control where I was to go. I did not yield. Each tug, push, pull only served to heighten my resolve that I needed a different path. I would not be controlled by anyone or anything ever again.

It was this choice that led me to spend the next fifteen years as a pauper. Hunger drove me to the brink each time. No matter what promises I made to myself, I surrendered time after time after time. I went mad with blood-lust, drinking every last drop. I lost count of how many fell at the tip of my fangs. None survived. Not one returned. I tried a couple of times, giving them my blood, seeing if they would change too. Women that would not be missed, but that might offer some friendship. Part of me was glad each time they remained lost. Would I ever feel right turning them into this? Would they have forgiven me when I had not forgiven Victor?

In the end, I was always alone. I taught myself to steal, only to realize one night when caught, that if I focused, I could just ask. People would give me things, assist me, forget me, with a direct stare accompanied by a few words. Few posed much of a challenge in this regard, but nonetheless, I was leery of getting greedy. Being known would mean discovery, which meant I would have to move on much sooner.

I had thought of my family often but could not bring myself to return at first. After a few years, the isolation became too great, so I did. I found the gravestone they had carved for me in the family plot. My date of death listed as the night I went to the convent. I knelt on the ground, the years alone flowing from my eyes. I wept for what could have been, who I could have been.

Carried on the wind, the alluring aroma tore me from the consuming self-pity. My legs carried me in a panic toward the house before I could regain my senses. Too late, I entered my old home to find Johnathon on the floor by the front door. His blank stare so foreign from the kind expression he held when he drove me home that night. In the kitchen, our cook lay beside our maid in one corner. They held onto one another; their faces somehow serene despite the stains covering their pale grey dresses. Each servant I found was now a shell of the person they were. Their throats were all ripped open savagely, the aroma of their blood lingering in each room. None appeared to have run far or fought. The final gift left with each was the faint scent of their murderer. One I memorized as I bore witness to their tragedy.

I found my father in his office upstairs. The fireplace popping as it devoured the fresh logs barely scorched. He sat in his favorite chair, facing the blaze. The paper was neatly folded in his lap, his crisp white shirt marred in a pattern of darkening crimson. On the floor was a picture of me. Drops of his blood had fallen on the lower half of the photo from his fingertips. He had been thinking of me. He had still loved and missed me. I froze, another drop landing on my neck in the image. Impulse bent me to pick it up and slide it in my pocket as anger began to boil within.

I surveyed each room, a secret prayer going unanswered when I crossed the threshold of my bedroom. When my mother lay eyes on me, she shakily raised her hands.

"I knew I would see you again when my time came. My Jenna. My angel. If I had only known then what price we would pay. I am so sorry. Will you ever forgive me?" Her words ceased when a fit of coughs racked her body. Blood expelled to land on my face, my lips. Instinctively, my tongue darted out to lick the blood away, a mistake I realized when I felt my fangs dart out. My vision took on a sharper view, and her voice cried out.

"Demon. Monster. How dare you take on my child's face? I hope he comes back. I hope he can find me in death, and I will agree to anything to see you destroyed. All of you destroyed." The more she spoke, the more the dark stream flowed from her mouth down her jaw. I could hear how slow her heartbeat was. She did not have much longer. I stayed at her side, my eyes direct on hers.

"You do not see a monster. You see only your daughter. Your Jenna. You do not feel pain." I struggled against the tidal wave of emotions washing over me. Worry that my current state would stop me from succeeding eased when I saw her sigh. She relaxed while I tensed. I could so easily lean down to savor the remaining essence that pumped beneath her flesh. It was her voice that banished the call to feast.

"Jenna, my darling girl. I am so thankful that I had you. Even if our time was cut short. I would do it all again. I would agree to have you, no matter what. You are all I have ever wanted." I did not understand my mother's words, not then or now. A dying woman's delirium, perhaps? She could not have known this would become of me. Could she? Agreed? Given our society, women were rarely given a choice. To bear children was our duty, one I realized I could no longer say was within my grasp.

Seated in a modest room, I glanced down at the body. He had been beating a woman, so I truly felt no remorse for his demise. His taste was not satisfying, but the hunger was again under control. If I could feel ill from a person's blood, I imagined his would do the trick. I had managed to resist the thirst for two weeks. I knew I could not delay longer, so I had waited until the perfect time to stroll the alleys tonight. This part of town never failed me. Men and women would linger amidst the cover of the shadows to do what the light of day would not permit.

I wondered if they ever thought they would end up prey to another. Dead on an aged brown rug beside a dinged-up metal framed bed in a hotel. I found places like these were best, to avoid attention. The place was clean but not maintained, which suited me when I rolled up the rug or sheet and had the body tossed into the river or the dump.

The men that took care of things for me never knew what they were doing, why, or for whom. This time, I had been using the same pair since I arrived here. Orders to stop by tonight were given before I had gone to hunt. I had been a customer for five months now and the amount of people missing was beginning to be noticed.

Another issue I continued to face over the years was the call. If I let my guard down for too long, that siren call became more enticing. I contemplated it. Where would it lead? Who was at the end? What did they want? Was it even real? Come. That's all I ever heard. To arrive where someone else wanted. Not a request, but a command. No, I would not be at anyone's mercy again.

I knew the energy of this person was always watching, waiting for a chance to take over my will. Yet the communication never seemed to work both ways. There were nights I called out asking what they wanted, who they were. That certain feeling that I could not explain told me they were a man. Was it Victor? One day, I would see him again. One day, he would die, one way or another. I needed to learn how to kill him first.

I thought about the girl I was, the dreams I'd had for my life. To be married, to have children, to have that perfect life that I had envisioned so clearly. To have been so certain of that future seemed now like a cruel joke. That Fate had been acting as nothing more than a traveling salesman selling tonic to regrow a man's hair.

A fly landing on the dead man's ear brings a sigh from between my parted lips. Perhaps this was why. I am now a monster that fed on a convent full of nuns, has killed countless men and women since, and will kill again. Somehow, I have restrained myself from ever killing a child. Even the monster I have become cannot seem to stomach that atrocity. From the murders at the convent to this dwelling, during the passing of years, I am left to ponder what else I was to do or lose myself to the madness of boredom.

CHAPTER 6
~ JENNA ~

The time had come to move on. I packed my trunk, going around the room to make sure I left nothing behind. Everything I traveled with fit within a large, worn, brown trunk and a suitcase. In truth, I could carry the heavy luggage, but I could not imagine how another would believe that such a feat was possible. So, I played the part. Once I was ready, I picked up my coat, stopping when a feeling I had never felt hit me. My head shot towards the door, my feet carrying me there a moment later. My hand grasped the knob, only to pause.

In fifteen years, there had been nothing new. There was a rush of excitement mixed with caution. Were my prayers answered, or was the one who called tired of waiting? Not another second wasted, I opened the door.

"You could sense me. Interesting. Lady Devereaux, I am Marcus Castillo. I will have my man attend to your things. We need to make haste if we are to depart unscathed." Much more than his stunning blue eyes kept my lips from moving. There was an aura that rolled off him in waves. Animal instinct sang out one word: Danger. His voice matched his presence, a slight gravely tone that no doubt caused most women to flush at a mere syllable.

"Do you truly expect me to accompany a man I do not know, Mr. Castillo?"

"I was asked to bring you somewhere safe. To teach you control and more, so that..." he pointed behind me, "does not happen again. At least, not unless you desire it to."

His eyes pooled with crimson yet swirled with streaks of black. He stepped back, hand outstretched as if to show me the way. There was no doubt that he would not take no for an answer. We stepped outside, where I saw the only carriage waiting, his.

"Presumptuous of you, Mr. Castillo."

"Not entirely. You were coming with me, one way or another. You are too inexperienced to have won in a match against me. Though I may have enjoyed your attempt."

"Very presumptuous of you." My tone was flat. I was not angered by his words, for I knew they rang true. My senses sized him up the moment our eyes locked. This was a fight that could end me. Going with him could end me. I did not care. I understood there was more I had not uncovered about who I was, and I saw him as a way to learn. A book to read then leave behind, once satisfied the pages surrendered their secrets. For better or worse, this was something new to break the solitude.

We entered the cabin as his men exited with my trunk, suitcase, and black cloth with the body underneath. I watched through the window; the trunk taken to the back, the suitcase secured on top, the body slung over a horse. The rider took off even before the last strap was fastened. The moment his man took the reins, the horses began to pull. Marcus sat forward to close the shutters over the windows. Sunrise was not for hours but I noted then that he looked weary.

I pondered on where we were going and if he had come from there to simply collect me and return. Why? How had he known where or who I was? Who had sent him? This man held power, so what must the requester hold? He sat back with his eyes closed, showing how little he desired to speak.

"Stare any longer, my lady, and I will take it as an invitation." Eyes closed; his voice seemed to echo off the thin walls that shook as we traveled down the road.

"Invitation?" I regretted the word spoken even as my lips ceased their movement.

In the blink of an eye, he sat beside me, his hand on my throat forcing me to angle my head to one side. I would not give him the satisfaction of asking for mercy if he was trying to scare me. All the anger I had bottled up about the first attack rose to the surface as I grabbed his wrist. I heard a crunching sound, but he did not relent. Instead, his tongue ran the length of the vein in my neck.

Then, as quickly as he neared, he was back on the other side, rubbing his wrist. He pulled and twisted on his hand with a resulting groan escaping from his lips. As he massaged it, the bruising that was just forming faded away.

"You are strong. I will give you that. Stronger than I expected a Turned to be. Especially one so young. Hell, I am surprised you survived the transition when most people do not."

I did not engage. I never had felt entirely normal, though what female did? His words, though, confirmed for me that this was done to me, not a previous part of me. When he spoke, I knew that to be true, but could not shake the sense that the puzzle remained incomplete, nor did I trust him.

He slept on our journey while I remained alert. I studied his features, the way his chest rose and fell almost imperceptibly, the scent of morning casting off the night deep in the forest, the mix of something I was unfamiliar with combining to trigger a prey emotion from deep within my chest. He was lethal. So, was he here to help or to use me?

With his eyes shut, the depth of the blue gaze I first saw

remained hidden. How it contrasted with his tanned skin, his hair a sun kissed light brown that was tied in a black cord at the base of his neck before disappearing into his coat. To others, he would appear a man who enjoyed leisurely days soaking up the rays. Glancing around the confined space, the absolute darkness created by the shutters told otherwise. I did not see him as one to walk in the day. Which once more raised the question, why could I?

That was just one of the many questions that gnawed at me over the years. One I had dismissed because I did not know how true any of the old stories were. Now, I wondered. Numb to almost everything, the anger over the life I'd lost boiled beneath the surface. I had often used this as justification for those who sated my blood lust. My prey of choice were men that I observed harming women or children, or even men weaker than them. Those who made themselves feel better by controlling those who could not or would not stand against them. It would serve me now in sharpening my focus, as I learned all I could from this man. So, I would know how to defend myself, and how to kill Victor when we meet again.

My comatose host knew of me, how much I could not say. Was he aware of those I fed on? Had he spies that told of the documents I influenced some to sign before I drank them dry? I owned many factories, brothels, and various other businesses that once belonged to the parasites I destroyed. Tips I picked up from eaves-dropping on my father's business meetings as a child. Women that once relied on their captors worked for me. A network forming with each new interaction. They gave me tips to satisfy my hunger, and I protected them. I would call none of them a friend. I kept communication between us at a minimum and most did not even know for whom they worked.

A bump rattled the carriage hard, jolting me from my thoughts. My companion stirred to straighten in his seat. He slid open the shutter closest to him. The faint light that dared to enter the narrow slit fell on his hand, which began to redden after several minutes passed. Curses were mumbled under his breath. Were there levels of tolerance? I walked in the sun constantly without any irritation, yet minutes in the sun made his burn like the time we had gone on vacation, and I had played too long on the beach.

CHAPTER 7

~ JENNA ~

When we arrived at his estate, I delayed entering, to take in my surroundings. We had traveled throughout the day, and the sun was already kissing the horizon behind the massive dwelling. Built entirely of grey stone, save for the black roof, and all the windows which were adorned with black metal framing. A stained-glass window depicting a phoenix rested above the large wooden door. Before we reached the threshold, the door swung open. An elderly man stood to the side to allow us to pass without a word.

Upon entering, I was quickly ushered to a room that was larger than the bedroom I had known. The bed was draped in a satiny crème duvet, matching lace was tied to each bedpost, and adorned with roses so deeply red that they appeared black from a distance. Candles were scattered about the room from the mantle above the fireplace to the bedside tables and vanity that were positioned near the window. Here too, the curtains had been tied back on each side, but they contrasted with the delicate nature of the decor. Black and heavy, they hung on separate poles that ran longer than the window as to permit them to cross, leaving no chance for sunlight to break into the privacy of anyone dwelling here. The floor, walls, and ceiling were all a soft tan color that gave a sense of warmth.

I walked around as my belongings found their way inside the double doors. I did not have to allow my attention to travel in that direction to know that Marcus stood there, studying me thoroughly. There would be time for him later. My intent was to learn if this was a regular occurrence. I saw no sign of another occupant having been here recently. Upon my examination, the room appeared to have been recently cleaned. Switching my focus solely to my sense of smell, I detected a faint musty odor in the air with faded notes of an older woman that had spent very minimal time here recently. Apparently it was she who prepared for my arrival.

"You can stop, Miss Devereaux. No one else is here but those who serve me. Among them, only three are human. Harm any here..." He stood tall, arms uncrossing to put his hands in his pockets, a move that should have made him less menacing but, caused the opposite effect. He did not need to finish, a fact he knew well enough as he turned to leave, closing the doors with a click.

I slowly put away my things, resigned that this was my temporary home. The task complete, I wanted to explore the rooms, see what might be of use to me. My progress halted at the doors that refused to open. A smirk played on my lips; harnessed strength resulted in nothing more than a rattle of the hinges. I heard a quick chuckle from the hall; I was locked in. The doors somehow reinforced against the strength I possessed.

"This is your first lesson. You will stay in there with only what I provide as sustenance. You must learn not to deny what you are, that leads to gorging yourself when the hunger becomes too much. This will be hell for you, but you will learn eventually. This way you can avoid detection or exposing us to humans. You've caught the attention of those who demand we remain in the shadows. Consider this your punishment and your only chance to avoid a fate far worse."

"Worse? Worse than being a monster? You must be mad. I will not stay here as a prisoner. I will be no one's victim, not now, not ever. Do you hear me? Never again!"

I heard steps approach the door, his voice a whisper for my ears alone.

"Jenna, you need to trust me. If not, at least trust that you are strong enough to survive this. To grow stronger through this process. You will hate me. That is ok. There is another I am doing this for. One I owe a debt to and one I refuse to fail."

"Marcus! Let. Me. Out."

I cried out, fists pounding on the solid wood to earn a couple splintering cracks that did nothing to release me. Faintly I heard his steps recede, then silence. I could not say how long I beat the drum to the tune of my anger. I was surprised to find tears blazing a path down my cheeks. Exhaustion claimed my body, the floor my bed. I leaned against a corner, unable to keep my eyes open another moment.

I woke in the night, my dress bunched up, legs curled to the right. My head leaned back, permitting me to take note of the red that stained the door. I had hit it so long and so hard that I broke the skin on my hands. I cast my gaze down to see the dried evidence coating them. There were no cuts or bruises beneath, at least no longer. I rose to wash with the thought of how my mother would be dismayed to see her daughter in such a state.

"Mother. Father. I miss you still." I sometimes wondered who had been the one to cut the strings on their fate. I held no illusion that it was anyone other than another vampire. His scent had been there, covering each body like a veil. When I had left, I set the place on fire. I could not stand the thought of them being found as victims of a monster. The last ties I had to my mortal life, nothing more than the ash part of me longed to become.

The water in the basin tinted a light shade of pink as I removed the dried blood. I imagined it the last remnants of the vampire who killed my parents. I thought such creatures must be rare; I was not so sure now.

Something about my current host plagued me. He was most undoubtedly a vampire, but his scent disturbed my instincts and left me shaken. The fight-or-flight survival instinct we possess rose in his presence. The feeling clearly screamed to me to run away, flee from him post haste. My stubborn streak refused to obey. Any risk he posed was pale in comparison to what I needed from him. My captivity was a setback I simply had not predicted.

I moved to stare out the window. The moon claimed the night sky. Shadows from the trees raced with the gloom of the large fence that I could see surrounding the property. Which would make their way to the house first? Was this to be my source of amusement? How long would I be constrained? I had to stay if I was to learn.

"I will survive this. Then I will find you."

Three weeks passed before I saw anyone else. In that time, the hunger grew insatiable. I screamed, kicked, cried, begged, but all attempts went unanswered. Every muscle in my body ached, constricted, tore, only to rebuild. My skin paled further, sweat soaked every layer I wore. No longer able to stand the weight of anything on my skin, I stripped, weeping as I hugged my knees to my chest. Red filtered my vision, my thoughts consumed with one thing and one thing only. Blood. I needed to feed.

Feeling feral, I wanted to kill Marcus. He brought me here just to torture me to death. To allow me to starve until I went mad or died. As if I willed him into being, he entered with no more regard than if he was walking into his own room. Which, in truth, I suppose he was. I did not care that I lay naked before him. I could smell blood. He carried a large golden goblet in his hand. My eyes would not leave the glistening chalice. I pounced, tore it from his grasp to permit the warm liquid to travel down my throat. In my haste, some spilled from the corners of my mouth, leaving red streams down my neck, flowing between my breasts to my abdomen.

My sanity returning with the edges of my hunger sated. I hated myself. How delicious blood tasted. How I longed for it, coveted it. The monster I had become desired more even now. I wiped my mouth, sucking the remnants from the tips of my fingers. I still hated myself. The way I longingly examined the cup as if I could will it to fill. Fixated, I was startled when I felt the blanket cover me.

I was an animal surveying the surrounding area, door shut, a man standing near the entrance to the bathroom. Marcus looked dismayed. I expected rage when he saw what I had done to the room. Once beautiful, broken pieces of wood littered the floor. The lace that was tied to each bedpost was shredded. The only unscathed cloth were the curtains that kept the sunlight barred from entering. Even instinct can filter into madness. If he were to seek me out, he would need to know it was safe. Though standing now, I examined the heavy fabric for signs the sun held its rule over the day. I could open them to free myself from this twisted game.

CHAPTER 8
~ JENNA ~

He nodded to the bathroom, then waited with arms crossed over his chest. "You will dress and accompany me while your room is sorted. Try to run or do anything I dislike and there will be consequences. Severe consequences. Do not test me."

The blood I consumed eased the hunger, but did little to provide strength. I was exhausted and elated at the notion of leaving this room for even a short while. I went into the bathroom, unfamiliar clothes shoved into my hands. I washed, brushed my hair before tying it back with a black ribbon, and inspected the clothing. Pants? He had given me men's pants with a fitted sleeveless top and a slightly larger white top that tied halfway down. I swallowed hard. I had never worn pants. My mother would not permit it. In my room, I had pretended several times but never in front of another. If mother had ever caught me, I would have been punished for my immodesty.

I slipped into the garments, turning to look at my reflection in the mirror only to have the image mock me. No longer did I see the remnants of the past. The tumultuous days confined, the way I savored the crimson liquid poured down my throat, it snuffed out the last ember of hope. If I was to survive, I had to drink.

Walking the halls, our steps were the only sounds to accompany us. I took in the decor along the way with mild interest. Some pieces that sat on pedestals made me think of the time my family went to a museum in London. Every artifact had been secured behind thick glass. These sat open and begged to be touched. The history they signified enthralled me, varying from the ornate to the plain. This was the first genuine spark of life I had felt in almost two decades.

Through the massive room I saw when we arrived, we headed to the corner at the far wall to the right. He pressed something on the wall, which made the bookcase swing toward us. Behind it was a dimly lit stairwell that curled out of sight. We descended slowly; the lights growing more scarce the further down we went. When I felt I could no longer see, I reached out to grab his hand. My hand clutched his while I wondered what new hell I was about to endure.

"Let go. This is your lesson. You can see far better than you know. Natural abilities are being blocked by you and your mortal notions of the possible. You did it in the carriage without thinking. Stand here until you can see the room."

"It is pitch black. I cannot see without light. No one can."

He yanked his hand free, leaving me slightly off balance. I corrected my balance before falling as his steps receded, though he remained. Father always said that fear could be the most powerful motivator. I was frightened, more than that, I was growing weary of these games. Why could he not just tell me? I wanted to know how I came to be. I wanted to know how many more walked the land. How could I find them? How could I kill them? How could I kill Victor?

"I can sense your emotions. You are not the only one who is not supposed to exist. Your fear is your true jailer. Your refusal to let go of your mortal life will be your executioner."

"What would you know? Is this how you find pleasure? Your idea of training someone is to torment them. To scare them into submission. I refuse to be your plaything, your toy." Memories of being locked up, his captive to be used, flooded my mind, but they brought my anger with them. My desire for vengeance.

"Stop fearing what you are." His voice came from every direction, soft and low.

"I am not afraid." I ground out.

"Liar."

"Ass."

He chuckled, an honest hint of surprise lending itself to his words. "Now, now. I had thought you were raised a lady."

"I am a lady. That does not change the matter at hand. That you, sir, are an ass." I was deflecting. I knew the tactic well, but that didn't stop the smile that curled one side of my mouth.

I bit my tongue hard enough to draw a small amount of blood. A minor distraction from the state I was in. He was correct. I loathed to admit it, but the reality of it shrouded us as surely as light failed to reach down here. Why was I fighting against this? I wanted to learn, to know more. So why? I supposed that the mind refused regardless of our wishes.

I shut my eyes, the voice within whispering to let go. Every chance I gave, the monster within rose, I felt it. Something else, something wickedly dark, clawed to take hold. Every experience cut short seconds before I surrendered to the energy oozing through the cracks of my resolve. Nausea swirled in my gut. My back felt oddly heavy, fangs elongated, tears that wished to release dried without a drop spilt. I feared the death I already died. I fought against the monster I already knew myself to be.

I was paralyzed at the notion that my existence was to be alone for all eternity. Now. Here. I feared the spark that whispered to me that I could live a life again. I danced along the cliff, teetered on the edge. With a scream, I opened my eyes to see. And I saw everything.

She was magnificent. The short time she had been in my care confirmed my suspicions that information was withheld when the request was sent. I was not one involved in other's matters. This was a fact all knew well, so when the request came that I collect a newborn to train personally, my curiosity was piqued. Of course, I would have refused, regardless, if the debt had not been brought into the matter. Then, when outside her door, her scent called out differently. I had never encountered a scent like hers. She was something new. I thought that to be impossible. Upon seeing her, I knew at once I was correct. This was a special case. She was special. The aura she presented was unlike anything I had experienced in all of my years.

There was no doubt that she was, at least in part, a vampire. More was hidden within her being. Her scent was intoxicating. If my will had not been honed over centuries, I may have nipped her when I licked her delicate skin in the carriage. Prowling around her in the dark, my predatory instincts demanded to be sated. One drop to uncover the mystery held just out of reach.

She stood with her eyes closed against the truth for over an hour. Time passed while she fought with a genuine acceptance of what reality now held. When her eyes surrendered, I could tell at once that she had done it. The windowless stone walls matched the stone floor and ceiling. They adorned a solid oak table at the front of the room with a rich, velvety black runner that hung almost to the floor. A silver thread of runes ran the length of the cloth. They held a message for me alone. Realization dawned in the bleakness of our surroundings that no other had seen the symbols in a century, at least.

I circled around her, assessing how she focused. Since her arrival, I had others investigate her background. From what I had been told, she had fought against her nature since she was bitten almost sixteen years ago. She decimated around forty nuns and a couple of priests when she awoke. In the years following, she refused to eat until her hunger became painful. Even then, she taught herself enough control to feed on those she deemed deserving. I could tell she does not know how much control she already had over her thirst. Admittedly, I found her to be impressive, though unbelievable. If I had known all this at the time of the letter, I may have taken her on even without the mysterious request. Maybe.

A letter sealed with black wax held the minuscule information I had to go on about her initially. Accompanying that letter was a note from one I trusted that simply warned this was an offer I could not refuse. The note went on to elaborate that in completing this task to satisfaction, all favors owed would be erased. Considering the two favors I had outstanding; this was no small feat. One notion gnawed at me from that moment to this night...who was so interested in this woman that they would go to such lengths? Who had the ability to do so? Why require this of me?

"Tell me what you see, Jenna." My voice was barely a whisper, yet I knew she could hear me as clearly as if I spoke directly into her ear. Her senses were awakened, not yet to their full potential, but enough now that she accepted what she was.

"I see stone walls rising from a stone floor. A large table with a cloth that has some intricate writing. There are a handful of paintings on the wall. You. I see everything as if the room was cast in the midday sun. I can hear a faint trickle of water, a stream running underground some ways off." She spoke like a child afraid to raise their voice for fear of being heard by their parents. Wonderment, curiosity, lingering uncertainty colored every syllable.

I moved closer, motioning her toward the other side of the room where the hallway brought us to a library much different from the one in the main living quarters.

"The books along these shelves keep secrets far older than any mortal eyes have ever seen. You must learn our ways, our history, what else exists in the world. You will not be allowed to say you did not know by the time we are done. Learning the customs and laws that you will abide by will take time. Some of these are diaries. Perhaps they will help you to see that we are not all monsters."

"Are you? A monster, that is?"

"That, my dear, depends on your definition." I paused, watching how she refused to look away from my eyes. A smirk spread across my lips in response. "By most, yes. I am a monster."

I shook my head, hand raised to cut off whatever words were ready to slip from her tongue. "You were a girl, living a lavish life when tragedy struck, yet I must confess something. There is more to you than a mere vampire essence. Your scent is alluring. Your blood, I have never smelled anything like it before. One day, I would like to drink from you."

"You say that as if such a request is common. Please pass the sugar. Oh, and a cup of your blood if you would be so kind," she scoffed, the sarcasm she held as a shield, firmly in place.

She moved to the first stack; her fingertips traced the spines of the volumes that lay beneath a blanket of dust. This may assist in providing the desired outcome. Knowledge is power. Control is essential. Combat will always be inevitable. These are the things she would learn if she wanted to go back into the world.

CHAPTER 10
~ JENNA ~

The books captivated my attention. Memories of sitting by the window with a volume of poetry in my hands flooded forth. No sunlight was to be seen from this room. No pillowed seat waited to pass the hours with the backdrop of rolling green meadows. The doorway from which we entered was the only passage to grant entry or exit. Accompanying the six bookcases lining the walls, four more stood floor to ceiling like columns, with a sofa and a small table in the very center of it all.

"Every time you have fed, you will be permitted to come here. Read whatever you wish. Stray from here or the main area of the house..." Marcus' deep voice trailed off, whether to leave the rest to my imagination or simply because he felt the rest went without saying. I did not know, nor did I care.

I ignored him. My purpose lay before me. Eyes scanned the titles in search of one that called out to me. There were so many. I was uncertain I would ever be able to read all of them. Walking around the stacks, I turned the corner to find him standing there with a rather large volume in his hands. Taking the book in silence, I opened the cover to feel the frailty of the secrets it contained. The leather-bound book held pages so brittle I feared they would crumble from the slightest touch.

"Start with this."

Within seconds I was seated on the sofa, the first words beginning to take me back to a time when stories were filled with princesses, dragons, and princes. This was certainly no fairy tale. No time was needed to realize this was a diary, one hand-written by someone who did not offer their name. I continued to learn that they were a boy, a teen raised on a farm by a father, alone with his younger sister. One the boy seemed to have been very protective over.

Page after page, I lost myself in the life of the stranger. Struggles of daily life, of the pressure to become the man who the family can rely on in his father's aging years. Even in their impoverished state, they too sought a marriage to improve the life of the only female under their care. They fought over who that man would be. The one in town demanded the honor, a more comfortable life but one without tenderness, without love, would be her fate. They agreed before ever telling her.

The dates skipped now and then; time untethered to the story unfolding. I learned of a boy who became a man. A brother that killed a man meant to protect the one thing he cared for. The night after his sister's funeral, he lay at her grave. Rain pelted the ground; he wished that the muddy earth would soften and allow his body to sink within its depths. He wished to disappear. To cease to exist. Yet vengeance snipped the cord of his despair.

Before his death, he coveted the death of the other, the man who stole the only good thing in his life. His father had passed a year prior, sickly, he succumbed to his only escape from a life of hard work, the only rest he would ever find. Dead, without knowing the depth of the mistake they had made. He was thankful his father did not have to carry the guilt of it with him.

He lay there, a sack of human flesh without the soul to move. The ground did give way, just not how the young man had prayed. Rocks fell from the hill to his back. Many found their final resting place against his still form. A clicking noise took to accompanying the rhythm of the rain. He remained as he was, his mind envisioned the reaper coming forth, his staff that noise which he welcomed. Death's call may allow him peace. His crazed mind imagined a ghost that tormented the recent widower.

"There are better ways to exact justice on the vileness of men." An unknown voice filtered in to join the orchestra of the night.

The man did not reply. Grief. Loneliness. Guilt. Hatred. It was the only language he knew now. He was dead inside. A living specter that did not want to admit that he would never obtain the revenge he sought. He felt a sodden cloak cover him, even damp, the fabric forced some warmth back in. Then the impossible. Lifted from his resting place, they carried him several meters from his sister to the trees. Here they were granted some shelter from the weeping sky.

"I have been bored. You will provide me some levity, or you shall die a simple meal. Either way matters not to me," the man's reaper declared.

He was bitten. He was found buried beside his sister, the ending to their family name. If only that had been the end, yet he returned. Turned into one of the monsters that hid within the night. Days later, the town discovered his grave disturbed, wooden casket ripped open. Legends began as some whispered how the grave appeared to have been dug up from within. All wanted answers, comfort to allow them peace. They turned to the new mayor, only he did not answer the call. His room was painted with a deep crimson splash. Parts of him were found throughout the home. Except one piece. His heart. That was never found.

The writing continued. It told of the way he often thought of that night. The way he felt tearing off the mayor's arms. The aroma that filled the air as the blood pumped free with each fading beat. All he saw were the bruises his sister wore, the melancholy tone her voice adopted with every passing year she spent with the man. How much worse that final year had become for her. His sister, the woman he knew, had ceased to exist long before her death. She had not wanted the marriage. She had begged for any other match. They only wanted what was best for her, believed her hysterics were that of a young woman unprepared to be wed.

Too late, he had realized the man they had given his sister to was far worse than they feared. They thought him cold, harsh, though never as villainous as the truth told. The death of the mayor was not a nightmare, but a dream. The writer saw the act as avenging his sister, atonement for having agreed to the match. Every kill after, he saw only one face, heard only one voice in the pleas that filled his ears. Blood that soaked his hands, skin that was packed beneath each nail, those were the memories that fueled his existence.

The more I read of his plight, the more I felt for the man. The heartbreak he endured was one that the greatest poets failed to capture with their flowery words. All the hours I lost myself to the prose of men long dead did not move me as this tale. I envisioned Marcus lying in the mud, the tears he shed. That was until I neared the end of the leather-bound confessional. The man talked about how he had chosen to end his life. A silver rope fashioned for him by a local blacksmith. He pondered if the silver would burn through his neck to behead him or if he would be saved by the transformation, by the sharp claws, teeth, and fur that he had accepted as his curse in time.

Marcus was not that kind of monster. Was such a thing even possible? I sat, uncaring of the time slipping away to permit my mind the freedom to imagine a sight as described. Werewolf. Werewolf and vampire. A laugh echoed off the stone walls that sounded completely surreal. The dawning washed over me as fully as the tide washes up over the shore. I was lost to the wonderment of if a werewolf and vampire hybrid could exist, as if such a fantasy were normal. That werewolves existed had not given me pause.

"Jenna Devereaux, thou hast officially lost your mind." The words filtered out on the last bubbled laughter leaving my lips.

Not knowing what time it was, I placed the book down and rose to make my way back to my room. I didn't sleep as much anymore, but I did still seem to require rest. Even more so when I had not fully fed.

When I reached my room, I pulled the heavy drapes open to watch the sun sink into the horizon. I had missed the entire day, lost to that diary of a man who became a monster to kill a monster. I sighed. The last glimmer of light was more vibrant than I had ever known before. Everything was. I knew tomorrow the sun would rise, another day of my own existence. No. Another day where I would live.

CHAPTER 11
~ JENNA ~

Days drifted into weeks, weeks into months, months into years. I had read three quarters of the books within the underground library. I was no longer subjected to the tortures of being starved, then fed like some pet.

"You cannot rely on your enhanced abilities alone, Lady Devereaux. They will do nothing against someone truly skilled with the knowledge of our kind." He often reminded me of this since training began.

I found more than the books, the training, and the solitude. I was learning about myself. A naïve woman of denial had birthed a woman of confidence. With that birth, a sharper tongue with quick words followed. Determination slowly replaced fear. The more uncertain I felt, the more I pursued achievement.

In a meadow to the south of Marcus' estate, we stood for another lesson. Not another soul existed for miles. As was now common, I dressed in pants with a loose-fitting top and boots. My hands were wrapped in what, at the start, was a bright white gauze. Both of us were now soaked in sweat, blood stains the only evidence either of us had landed a blow to the other.

Upon our first training session, if that is what one could call it, I was merely a pathetic thing to be taunted. He never broke a sweat or even had a single hair out of place. I, on the other hand, was scraped up from falling or getting flipped over for hours on end. I was sore for a short while after he had relented. By the time I arrived back at the house, a warm bath had already been drawn for me. While I sunk into the depths, I vowed one day I would best him, if only to no longer suffer the smug expression he wore.

I hoped today would be that day. Staying low, I used my smaller size to my advantage. We were a mere meter apart. Each of us stepped around the other. He knew I would attack, so he waited for me to do so. Too many times, I would give some tell as to how and when I would strike. I recited his words in my mind: do not step back for leverage before leaping forward, do not look where you wish to strike, do not overthink, act. Act. Here I was again, thinking. As he frequently stated, I am a hunter; I have instincts I must trust.

I dove forward, intent on grasping him by the midsection, lifting, then throwing him over to land behind me on his back. My hands clasped just barely behind each of his thighs, my head by his hip. I lifted to hear a huff of air leave his lungs. Was that a chuckle? A triumphant sensation filled my body while he left the ground. In the fraction of the second the move took, I stood with a smile plastered across my lips.

My elation sank faster than a stone into the nearby pond. Impossibly, boots sounded solid against the ground behind me. I turned in time to catch his arm across my neck. Air became a luxury I no longer afforded. His training paid off in driving my instincts, my leg kicked out on my way down. I mentally reveled in the one minor victory when he stumbled.

Once more I was reminded that my life shall never again be what I expected. I had kicked so Marcus would fall back. I had seen his body begin its descent. So how? I looked up at Marcus hovering over me. Marcus was close enough that our breaths mingled, his body almost completely covering mine. A glint of silver from a dagger he did not hold before reflected in his eyes as it pressed into my skin. A defiant air filtered into my thoughts. His words from when I first arrived bit back to bring my head down enough to just barely puncture the delicate barrier.

"This is what you want, right? To taste my blood? I have observed you eyeing the droplets before, when we have fought. So why not partake?" Truth would add that I wanted him to taste me. Marcus could answer why my scent or essence was unique.

"No!" The word exploded from his lips.

His body went rigid, his gaze swirled with the red and black depths I was growing accustomed to during our lessons. I was aware that a droplet of my blood traveled down the blade. His eyes grew darker as they darted between mine and the temptation. He appeared paralyzed, well, most of him. Along my hip, a hardness swelled.

Shock threatened to break my resolve. Memories of the past flashed. All I read, the training I completed, nothing cast away the shadow around why I was a target, why I was different. The thought had been forming for days, impulse brought it to reality. In a second, he was standing, so I rose to face him. Only his attention remained lower.

I took a step closer, the trail down the column of my throat the only evidence of the wound already healed. Marcus lifted the cold steel to his mouth, tongue surrendering to the desire for a taste as if he were entranced. The moment the gleam returned, the dagger dropped. A powerful arm was around my waist, that final crimson path cleaned entirely. His eyes morphed into a whirlpool.

The folly of my actions was apparent. One drop was not enough or perhaps it was too much. Marcus' fangs grew longer.

His attack was lightning quick. In that instant, several thoughts fought for dominance. Could I die if he bled me dry? Could I change more from another bite? From what I learned, yes to the former, no to the latter.

Panic roared from within, one thing was certain, I wished to live. Was I now to die? Then it happened. There. Gone. The ground marred. Marcus' blood expelled with each cough he let loose while on all fours a couple of meters away.

"What the hell?" He questioned, but I had no answer to give.

"I... I..." No words would follow. The scene replayed over again in my mind, provided nothing. I felt fear, genuine fear for the first time since arriving. Weaved within that fabric was something else. The fear was not simply for what I had done, but what I might do. Nothing in the countless tomes my eyes had engulfed, nor the scarce information Marcus relinquished, spoke of such an occurrence.

Marcus rose. The back of his hand smeared the ruby essence from his lips. His eyes bore into me like he was seeking a change, another cause for the surge that sent him flying backward. Seconds passed without a word, his gaze memorizing each inch of my body. There was no lust reflected in the ocean blue of his eyes.

Exhaustion worse than anything before washed over me, preceding a blinding pain that started from within my chest and traveled along every vein. I cried out in anguish, eyes clamped shut against the world. I wanted to retreat to find some relief. Instinct screamed to cut off from everything until I could dull the ache that threatened to tear me apart.

Marcus was near immediately. His fingertips brushed my back, wrenching another scream from between my parted lips. Barely a whisper of a caress sent my nerve endings off with a fresh round of lightning, caged in blood and bone. I knew I was not going to die. Instinct told me I broke some barrier long held in place by ignorance. Knowing I was not one for the mortal world, as I had discovered it was called, was the key to dismantling this dam. The flood was now cleansing away the false landscape before it.

"**S**he's awake." A voice cut into the silence. The figure did not attempt to fully enter the chamber to deliver the news. The two words were more than enough to relay all that was needed.

Long, thin fingers tapped the armrest where he sat. The faint glow of light cast off the shadows enough to reveal a menacing smirk on lips that enticed one's gaze to linger. His straight black hair could be seen where it rested just below his shoulders. The fireplace in front of him danced, greedily devouring the logs he had recently added. He drank from the glass in his other hand until the amber liquid was gone.

At last, he stood, walking to a table along the wall to his left. He was tall, lean, his black suit fitted to reveal perfectly sculpted muscles that lined his entire body. The shadows shrunk along the floor as if to move from his path.

His plan was coming together. The vampire nearly ruined everything. He thought for certain he would have to wait another thousand years for the opportunity to try again, but she lived. Not only did she live, but she also maintained that which was of use to him. He had yet to confirm that all was well. His patience could be as enduring as necessary. Besides, he did not wish to make another arrangement with them if he did not have to. It seemed he was right to bide his time, after all.

He knew what those words conveyed. She tapped into her true essence. She would not understand what she was doing or how. Even her dear teacher, Marcus, would be in the dark about how she was capable of anything she did. That was by design. There had never been one like her and there would never be again.

"My little Jenna. Grow. Ripen. Become strong, my sweet." He spoke to himself, fingers tracing the ancient text only one other had ever seen. The scribe was no longer of this world, a thought that made his smile widen.

When the time came, he would collect her. She had resisted his call urging her to him when she first transitioned. Over the years, he had tried other times, to no avail. He at last had the idea of sending someone to fetch her, train her, prepare her for what he needed. He found the only other who might come close to matching her strength when she awoke. Meticulously, he set all the players in motion, then waited. Waited for those two words: She's awake.

CHAPTER 13
~ MARCUS ~

I sat in my chambers; amazement whirled with frustration. Her taste was thrumming through my veins even now. My body was more charged, my senses heightened. My own nature at war within. I had mastered what I was so long ago, now the only thing my mind could agree on was blood. Her blood. I had tasted every manner of creature in my time, none compared to the adrenaline-fueled rush at hand.

I had to get away from her so I left her there on the ground before making another attempt. Despite that cowardice, I watched her from the window. She stayed there on the ground for hours, first with fits of pain, then what I could only assume was weariness from the ordeal. I assumed she came inside; I had turned away to discover that when I looked again, she was gone.

If only to prove to myself that I was the master of my mind and instincts, I barreled from my room toward hers. I wanted answers. My temper flared. Surely, she knew of her nature. She held secrets, lied to me, made me the fool.

Not. In. My. House.

There was no knock; the doors opened with such force they bounced back from the walls as I walked across the threshold. She was there, sitting on the edge of the bed, staring at her hands. She looked small. Immediately I calmed. With my agitated state, I could see something I only faintly recalled before. She had an aura around her that shone brightly, on full display for my demonic eyes.

"What the hell are you?" I asked, more to the aura than to her. Nonetheless, Jenna's chocolate eyes left her palms to meet mine. Only her eyes were not merely those deep brown orbs I had come to know, red swirled within them, then dissipated. Inky black pools consumed the bright red. This was not the demonic essence that swirled within my own, this was different. An abyss, but one with a question.

The allure they presented made me wonder what lay on the other side. For some, heaven or hell, torture or pleasure, to transform their energy or simply dissipate into nothing. Whatever one believed, the doorway currently stood open before me. A demon. A vampire. A hybrid. Without warning, a pinprick of light blasted from the center of each eye until they glowed brightly.

"What the fuck?" My arm shot up to shield my gaze lest I go momentarily blind. My body froze in place until the room was plunged back into darkness.

Jenna panted heavily; breath forcibly dragged passed her lips. Bloody tears ran down her cheeks. I was not tempted by the teasing stream this time. I moved to her, picking up a cloth from the nightstand to wipe them away. She shook in my arms, tremors rolling through her that I did not know how to console. For the first time in my life, I was out of my depth.

"I do not know. I swear it. I do not know." She kept repeating the words as though they may make the answer appear.

Over the last couple of weeks, she had been making real progress. Her training was coming along slowly, but her studies were impressive. The rate at which she read the volumes, the inquiries she made, the deductions she reached on her own. I was reluctant to admit that I had begun to enjoy having her there. A traitorous thought broke in as we sat there with her hushed oath. Was she sent to destroy me? A perfectly designed trap to finally end me?

The extinguished fire of my rage sparked back to life. I turned her by her shoulders to force our gazes on one another. All of my accusations sat like arrows on the tip of my tongue. Each pulled back, ready to hit their target.

"Jenna, who sent you to me? Who have you spoken to in our world that would have wanted us to meet? You cannot be so naïve. I know you have sought answers to your own questions, so you must have thought back on who in your life may be tied to what you are now."

Her eyes held mine, confusion fluttering across her features. Her skin, once porcelain white, now held a soft, sun-kissed glow. Dried tears had left pink streaks through the dirt that had laid claim, her lips were parted as she regained control of her breath. I realized in that moment that I had never truly seen her. She was an obligation, a means to clear the markers I had, and a way to pass the days that rolled into each other.

For a moment, I forgot my interrogation in favor of a memory. A woman with blonde hair, freckles adorning her nose, and the bluest eyes that made the oceans and the skies jealous. The way she would look at me, her youth fading with the years we had spent together. She had known what I was, yet only saw me as a man, as her man. How long ago had that been? Others had shared my bed for a night or two since, but nothing longer. How long had I even permitted that luxury? As if my body had a mind of its own, my pants grew tighter, the heavy weight pleading to end the confinement.

"Do not touch her." A voice cracked through my skull that caused me to press my palms to the sides of my temples.

I caught a glimpse of concern on Jenna's face, her hands rose to mine. The instant they made contact, the pain vanished.

CHAPTER 14
~ JENNA ~

He appeared to be in so much anguish. I attempted to inquire about what was wrong, yet my words could not seem to reach him. I placed my hands on his when a wave of tension seemed to wash away. He clasped his hand on mine as if he were drowning in a sea and had just found a rope. My hand was so small in his. The way he held on, fingers stroking the pulse point at my wrist made my breath catch.

A heat rose to my cheeks, my hands rushed to them to wipe at the already dried stains they wore. I cleared my throat; his initial questions grounded me as I wondered what was wrong with me. I latched onto those to avoid the trail my mind began to carve out. He was correct. Over the last year, I had begun dissecting all I knew. Why had that vampire been at that party? Who had invited him? Was it a plan for us to meet? Who called to me these last eighteen years? That last question I had never voiced to Marcus.

Being here made me believe I could learn to forge a life for myself. Granted, the purpose I set was the death of all other vampires. I desired sparing any others from succumbing to the same fate as me. I wanted revenge for the life I had lost, even if it was not to be. Revenge for my family. Revenge for every person who had suffered.

"I wish I knew." I was honest with him. "I have thought of that night often. Why that vampire was there? Who would have wanted me in his path or him in mine? There is no one that I can say is to blame. I so want to blame someone, to place their name at the top of my list, find them and ask them why before time steals my chance."

"I believe whoever has set this in motion is not one to be overcome by time." Marcus' voice held a slight gravelly tone. One that I had come to recognize meant he was weary, yet I did not want him to go. A question I could not halt slipped from my lips and caused him to stiffen.

"What did I taste like? My blood. I know from our training sessions we can tell the difference between species. You have even taken to quizzing me on them to no end. I do not know if it is because it is my blood, but I cannot discern what mine tastes like."

Marcus' eyes left mine to settle on the column of my neck. When at last he spoke, his voice was strained.

"The sweetest fruit and the deepest Hell. Your taste is unlike any I have savored before. Now, I have no doubt I will recall it until my death. I will crave it, and I will fear it."

Confusion bloomed. What did he mean? His response failed to answer what I had hoped. Before I could inquire further, he was gone. Alone, I sat on my bed thinking of everything that transpired.

"What am I?" I cried out in frustration.

CHAPTER 15
~ JENNA ~

I did not see Marcus for two weeks. Every time I went to his room, he was not there. I searched the entire estate, even during the day, he was nowhere to be found. The only servant I saw was a shy older woman that permitted me to feed on her. I had asked after him, only to be told that she did not know his whereabouts. Her only instruction was to remain on the grounds in case I was in need.

It had taken a full year before his torments of starving then feeding me ceased. I learned to control both my hunger as well as my feeding, so I did not have to kill. The final test had been most vile. A month. An entire cycle of the moon passed before I was permitted to feed. No cup was offered. Instead, a man was brought into my chambers. A man, I was told, who was a criminal scheduled for death. The desire to bleed him dry from thirst and justice was almost unbearable. However, I won. I stopped myself before I drank too much. My hunger sated; I released my grip to push him toward Marcus.

The pride he held in his eyes was unmistakable. Pride that I felt within at the same time. I was a little less the monster I was made to be. I had since counted the days until I might leave. My countdown now changed to when I might see him again. There was guilt. Had I driven him away? Why was I anxious that he may send me away? Much more needed to be taught.

I went to the library. The pages sprawled before my eyes were read three times. My mind saw only that day replayed countless more. The same as every day since he had gone. On a few occasions, my thoughts stumbled over when we were seated on my bed. The moment right before the despair crossed his features. Where was his mind? The expression was one I did not expect. One I knew all too well, but not one I had much experience with.

A tenderness I had not seen in years prior. A longing that stirred the same within. A curiosity I had never satisfied since Victor destroyed me. In the darkness, I considered my life. I would never have children, the family I dreamt of. Nor would I marry. Never would I have a wedding night. Was that to mean an eternity alone?

I had not thought of intimacy in all the years following my own transformation into a monster. If I spent too much time near a human, hunger would rear. The loss of my family. The vile nature I was aware of now existed within the world. Survival. The sensation that threatened addiction when my fangs sank into soft flesh to release that sweet elixir. Blood. The mere recollection of it flowing over my tongue. How the crimson flood soothed the parched plains of my throat time after time.

A pink hue colored my cheeks. One volume from the library spoke of a feeding being similar to sinking his shaft into the tight channel of his companion. The euphoria of the moment. The detailed depiction lasted a full page and a half. I saw the scene play out in my mind as I read his words. I was a voyeur, captivated by them together, wrapped in the most private embrace.

How many nights had I spent in the darkness of my room as a girl, imagining Trent and me in the same state? My fingers had traced along my body in exploration. They were his fingers, his mouth, his manhood. I would bite my bottom lip to keep anyone from hearing my cries or my promise that one day, we would be together. One more piece of my carefully planned life that would never be.

"What the hell is she?" My voice rattled the windows of the office. Dwight's desk had been smashed in two, his chair pushed near the wall in the corner. Books that I knew the man had never read lined the bookcases behind the wreckage. The facade so well established over years had been destroyed in less than an hour.

I punched the wall next to the trembling man's head. Wood splintered; bloody cuts healed before my hand fell back to my side. The plump older man appeared as if he might pass out at any moment. I leaned in to command his focus. The man's lips parted and shook with whimpers of words that failed to form. Once more, I bellowed the same question I had been asking for the last fifteen minutes.

"I... I... I don't know. I swear it. Marcus, I told you. I received a note with two packages. One to keep until Lucifer's Fire came to collect it. One with payment for me to forgive your debt and send you the letter of endorsement."

"That must have been a hefty payment." I paced away from the man.

"The note was more influential. Whoever requested your involvement knows of my entire family. Family that I have supported without claiming. A son who does not even know my name, Marcus." The man was on the verge of tears, unclear whether from fear or regret.

"Dwight, look at me. Really look." I moved back to the man that was now seated in a dark green tufted chair near the wall. "Do I look like I give a horse's ass about a single poor soul unfortunate enough to share your bloodline?"

Dwight was known to many. He was an *introducer* as he preferred to be called, or when more discretion was necessary, the man in the middle. He had some very powerful friends, which was the only reason he had survived so long. Many believed he had something on those friends, to garner such protection. When most in the area needed something, they chose between two options. There was Dwight, or for those permitted, there was The Agora. Unfortunately for me, I lost access to the services at The Agora for the very reason I owed such high favors.

I considered the minuscule information Dwight provided. Another letter. Another black seal. Unlike me, Dwight kept the envelope. I snatched the vile object. Someone was messing with me, and that was something I did not tolerate. Ever. My eyes scanned the seal. This imprint was unfamiliar to me. I knew all the family crests for every species, at least I thought I did. Wings perhaps. What may have been a stone of some kind. Dwight had not been kind when opening the envelope. The top right portion was lost, and what remained was a puzzle impossible to solve.

My fangs pushed out behind my lips. I craved a sweet nectar that was now half a day away. A temptation that I had no doubt could finally be the death of me. I just had to unmask who was trying to use this training as a means to my undoing. A grin pulled my lips to the side. A dagger I had hidden in the back of my belt was granted freedom.

"You will send word. Every high-ranking family, no matter the clan, is invited to a party at my estate. You will also send a tailor to fit myself and my guest with the latest fashions. I want her in white. They may accent the dress however they see fit. Just make certain they bring all they need. One month from now, on the night of the new moon."

"What if they do not wish to attend?" The quiver in his voice caused my grin to widen.

"They will come. I have not had a party for a hundred years. They will be curious. While they are there, I will put the little bird on display. I will see who takes a particular interest in her, how they accept her presence, and how they react to my proximity to her. Someone thinks I am a fool. I know when a string is being tied, but I will be no one's puppet."

I recalled the searing pain when my body reacted to her. Not really her, but the memory of another, of longing. Few had the ability to cause pain like that, fewer still that could sense what one was experiencing around one particular soul. I would force them to make themselves known, one way or another.

"Oh, and Dwight." I lowered myself until my face was near the now glistening brow of the man gripping the arms of the chair tightly. "Do not think to let slip a word of my intention."

"Never. I will take it to my grave." He replied, the force of his grip causing his knuckles to turn white.

Without warning, the dagger I held sliced through the man's hand and splintered the wood beneath. Dwight's scream pierced the air, receding only to crescendo when the steel was twisted free from his flesh. Blood poured over the top of his hand and through the hole in the armrest he refused to relinquish. He knew not to move. Tears streamed down his face as fast as the siren flow left the gash in his hand. His breath was a prisoner of his chest at the sight of me licking the blade clean.

"You are lucky you taste disgusting." My nose wrinkled as I slipped the gleaming steel back into its sheath.

With a tip of my head, I made my way out while I whistled.

He was home. I had feared that he may never return, or that when he chose to do so, I would be cast out. He was not the reason I chose to stay. I simply was not foolish enough to believe I was ready for the world. The opportunity to read more of the books in the underground library was tantalizing, but I also required more training.

That is where I sat now. A book in my hands that spoke of a council of elder vampires. The journal was more of a record. Family names, ten in the beginning, now just seven. Three of the families were wiped out in disputes, or by judgment from the council due to indiscretions. One I could scarcely believe, happened a few thousand years ago. The family was put to death for trying to enslave werewolves. The battle that ensued from their treachery cost many lives on both sides, along with collateral damage to mortals.

Wolves and vampires alike were left on stakes in fields. Heads, hearts, limbs scattered the ground. Blood made the soil soft, clinging to every foot that trespassed over the carnage. An agreement was reached to bring about peace. A safety none have threatened since. The council presides over all vampires, yet only interferes if one breaks the rules to extreme levels, or there is involvement from those outside the vampire specie.

As needed, the council still met at The Agora. That place sounded interesting. Powers are suppressed. Any attempts to cause harm are immediately stopped. The only other mention about it was that it had been run by one being known as The Host. No one ever sees them, but there is a family that serves as his representatives. The Thomas family had been in his service for generations. I wondered what they got from the arrangement, or if they were enslaved in some manner. More proof that there had been an entire world right under my nose that I never imagined.

When Marcus arrived home, he mentioned that the remaining council was invited to a party he was hosting. I wondered what I may discover from them. Would a representative from The Agora attend? How many would attend? I had to admit that my curiosity was piqued. How similar to the social gatherings of the elite would this be?

Tomorrow, I must meet with a seamstress. The first day where I am not required to assist with the preparations that consumed our days for the last two weeks. Tables with grey tablecloths and sheer white lace surrounded by plush grey chairs filled the room. The chandeliers were polished to a radiant shine, everything to his exact specifications.

His limited staff meant we both had to step in. Another new experience I had never considered, yet one I found enjoyment in. From what I witnessed; Marcus preferred to be involved in every aspect. Attending to so many affairs, the work that went into setting them up, astounded me. No time was permitted to dwell on my apprehensions, especially with Marcus keeping his distance. As it was, mild exhaustion demanded I wash, then get some rest before the new day.

No sooner had my eyes closed than a knock sounded at my door. Lingering dreams surrendered to the sound of the door opening. Feet shuffled in toward the heavy curtains that opened to grant entry to golden rays. I sat up begrudgingly, the back of my hand rubbing sleep from my eyes.

"Is sleep no longer allowed?" I did not try to hide my disdain.

"Lady Devereaux, you have slept for six hours. The seamstress is here and waiting for you to get ready."

I groaned, wondering how the time had slipped away. In truth, I was not weary any longer, just wished for momentary solitude. Knowing that was not going to happen, I rose and dressed while the petite blonde maid went to fetch the seamstress.

Standing in the brilliant light while I waited, I heard their footsteps coming down the hall. Noting the hesitation, the quickening thrum, I smiled as I turned. I knew what made her jaw slack, her pulse kick. I stood without harm in the warmth of the sun. She was a plump woman, brunette hair pulled back, a modest dress designed for style that allowed her the freedom to move with ease. It was gray, with black stripes going up and down her body.

"Well, I am quite certain this dress won't magically appear. Where would you like to begin?" My words laced with the hope that I could complete this task and then spend time on the patio with another book.

As she nodded, her feet hustled forward, a large bag plopped on my bed, from which she pulled out a measuring tape. She measured every curve along with my height. That which I knew, but had the absurd wonder if it had changed with everything else.

Peering over her shoulder, I saw that it had not. I would forever be five foot seven inches tall. The only difference I had been able to recognize was the increase in my bust, my bottom, and the toning of all my muscles. I was never large, but I had substance. Now, I had definition that I had even admired in the mirror. Those enhancements, I attributed to the trainings that had occupied much of my time.

When she had all that she required, she quietly said she would have the dress ready for me to try on in two days' time. Before I could inquire further, she scurried from my room.

"You should eat, my lady." I refocused on the voice I heard to find the maid standing with her arm outstretched.

She was right, I was hungry. I also knew that she despised having any feed from her neck. She was disgusted by us feeding on her at all, but seemed to resign herself to that chore. Dust the shelves, make the beds, have your blood drained as necessary. Some days, I still found it surprising that this was all so normal now. I wondered many times why she remained. Out of respect for Marcus, I never inquired.

Moving toward her, I clasped her forearm, my fangs elongated instantly. I bit into the supple skin; warm liquid coated my tongue. Her taste was sweet, reminiscence of the peaches I would sneak from the kitchen as a child. Who knew that blood could taste so delicious?

CHAPTER 18
~ JENNA ~

The night of the party, I reluctantly slipped into the dress that was made for me. A deep v cutting down the front was mirrored in the back. That alone made the gown the most risqué thing I had ever worn. Yet, the challenge against what I thought was appropriate did not end there. About an inch from the floor, the skirt ended. The gap permitting the silver-colored shoes to catch flickers of light. The fabric, a pearlescent white, came out a little at my hips with sky blue crystals woven delicately throughout.

If this had been a dress given to me nearly twenty years ago, I would have fainted at the thought. Now, I studied how I looked, realizing that I felt strong, nearly fierce. Downstairs many beings, nay, people, arrived. These were my people. I was part of their world. I would attend as one of them.

Marcus would see that I had earned the right to train more. My dream for my future changed from marriage to a man of honor, to learning to fight. Learning all the things I do not know of who these people are. Then, to kill all those who would harm innocents. This gave my life meaning.

With that thought securely in mind, I exited my room to find Marcus waiting there. Déjà vu brought an unladylike snort forth. He appeared to understand, a smile easy on his lips. He lifted his elbow in offering. That same familiar warning sounded, just as it had that first time we met: Danger. Nonetheless, as I did then, I accompanied him toward the stairs. I was surprised when he stopped at the top of the double staircase to clear his throat.

"Good evening. Thank you all for attending tonight. I promise you will not regret it." He pulled me closer to him, all eyes watched, waited for him to continue while I suddenly felt like the fox on one of my father's hunts. "I would also like to take this opportunity to introduce my special guest, Jenna Devereaux. Now, let the festivities begin."

Marcus stepped away with a glance and gestured for me. My arm linked with his, we headed down the stairs. One by one, people came to say hello, make introductions and superficial small talk. Before long, I forgot that all here were anything other than normal people. The only difference that stood out resided in the lack of conformity.

There were most assuredly rules for politeness and respect, but no hint of judgment for the dress I wore or what others wore. Some women wore suits, though more decorated than what the men wore. Some wore dresses of fashions I had only heard about from other parts of the world. Most of the men were in suits, some wore robes, and a couple were in kilts. The more I talked to them, observed them, the more fun I found myself having.

Then the dancing began. Marcus had hired a small orchestra group to play for the evening. Everyone took to the floor at some point. The music would range from traditional to music I had never heard. Men kicked their legs up then dropped down like they were sitting only to alternate kicking their legs more to the beat. What I knew to be a tango played for a second time. I stood there, watching them dance with my bottom lip caught between my teeth. This was a dance I had never learned. One I could not take my eye from.

"Come." Marcus spoke, but it wasn't a question.

I began to explain I did not know the steps, only to fall silent with his index finger against my lips. I heard his voice in my head, another training tactic we had been working on, but one I lied about. Each time I told him I did not hear him. Now, like each time before, I heard him clearly. "Just trust in me and follow my lead."

Bracing my arms as I had seen the others do, I obeyed. We moved slower than the rest at first. His movements keeping us in time with the melody that I felt in every inch of my body. Our steps brought us mere inches from one another. He dipped me back, my body arching against his while his head dipped to run his nose from my breasts to my neck as he pulled me up.

I felt heat bloom within my core, desire clamping down with an ache that I knew he could sense. A smile spread across his lips, faltered briefly, then remained in place. He did not take his eyes off mine. His hands traveled, one to tangle in my hair, the other wrapping around my waist. He squeezed tightly.

His lips were not gentle when they crashed into mine. They were hungry, determined, controlling. His tongue demanded entrance that I freely gave. Several times he tensed, then eased further into the kiss.

When we broke free of each other, I half expected to find others staring, whispering about what had occurred. There was nothing. All in attendance continued as though my breath had not just been stolen, or that the thief was not now holding my chin to make me look at him. I saw the lust in his eyes, or perhaps I saw a reflection of my own feelings. He tilted my chin up a little more, this time his mouth gently pressed to my own for a few seconds before he pulled back with a smile and whispered.

"That's my girl."

CHAPTER 19
~ MARCUS ~

As expected, when I touched her there was another angered by the proximity. A war waged but failed to penetrate whatever wall she constructed. I realized the moment I claimed her lips that she really had no clue. The way her body softened into mine, her tongue moved to taste me as I did her, the soft moan I don't think she even realized vibrated through her throat. If she knew another was in tune with her emotions, with her needs, or what others needed of her, she did not show it. There was no hesitation once she surrendered.

My body sprang to life at the images in my mind. At once, I wanted everyone to leave so I could test just how far she would give herself to me. This was not the plan, but having her? Yes. Too long had passed since I had sated that particular craving. The rational part of me scolded impatiently. Study. Observe. Uncover.

I walked her back to mingle among the guests before I parted ways. The heavy weight that had risen twitched in disagreement. I schooled my frustration with a promise that release would soon come. A glance over my shoulder made my mouth quirk to one side. Yes. Release would come many times tonight.

A drink acquired from the bar would do for now. I spent the next several hours in meaningless conversation with everyone from the local coven, to the heads of many werewolf families, shifters, demons, vampires, and even a single angel that graced my home.

My senses tracked her, no matter who I was with. No one approached her with concern. No one appeared upset with her in any way. Some made introductions, no doubt inquired about how long she had been turned, how she was turned. The obvious fact remained that they could all sense the difference in her. The slight way they sniffed, touched her arm, squinted at her. Did no one here really know what she was?

My body reminded me that part of me did not care at all what she was, only that she was here. That kiss meant to rattle the chain of the one linked to her had backfired somewhat. Either the years of abstinence or knowing her taste, I really did not care. I envisioned tearing that dress from her body and driving into her right there in front of everyone.

"Fucking hell." The words ground out under my breath.

I liked Jenna. She was kind. Her wonderment of all she was learning brought life back into my own, and she was gorgeous. Full breasts were moderately on display in the deep cut dress I had insisted on. I wanted her to shed any residual modesty the mortal world imparted. I found I enjoyed the borderline torment in forcing her out of her element to see how she would react. She told me she would never again be someone's victim; I learned she meant it.

If I could feel honest guilt, I might have. Tonight, she danced to the music, as well as the strings of puppeteers she could not see. Her mysterious guardian and I were now engaged in a game, with Jenna the only piece on the board. As far as toys went, I could think of worse ones to play with.

Guests had been taking their leave for the last hour, soon they would all be gone. The house once more left to me, my servants, and Jenna. The thinner the crowd became, the nearer I got to her. A sharp pain cracked through my skull; my hands flew to my temples in a futile attempt to shove the intrusion away. Jenna stood a few steps away. Her eyes widened when they fell on me. She rushed to my side, her hand on my arm, immediately succeeding where I had failed.

"Are you alright?" Concern. Genuine concern for me shone brightly.

I nodded and wrapped her hand around my arm at my elbow to keep contact. To her or others, a simple gentlemanly act. Reality, my shield to guard from further interruptions. My plan had progressed, now my reward.

The last guest gone; we made our way up the stairs in silence. I was hundreds of years older than her, but she was no child. Innocent? No, but not by choice. Child? No. I knew she had to consider what might happen when we reached the top. My room or hers? Would we pretend nothing happened? Like hell, I thought.

"Did you enjoy yourself, Jenna?" I broke the silence.

"Oh, yes, very much. To think all these people were around my entire life, but I never knew." She kept her eyes forward, only turning when we stopped in front of the large painting that hung on the wall at the top.

I considered how I might take her, test her, push her into submission. Not much caught me off guard, but she did. She took my hand, pulled me near to banish all plans from my mind. Our mouths spoke without the need for sound. Her tongue requested entry that I gladly permitted. I devoured her. Her taste, the feel of her smaller body, caught between mine and the wall.

Instinct took over. Desire. Need. Want. I gripped the strap of her dress; in a flash, the fine fabric became a tattered mess. Her skin beneath held that familiar pale hue unblemished by the sun.

I leaned back to admire her breast, her nipple a hard, rosy bud that pleaded for my touch. My hand shifted from her hip to cup the heavy mound; the peak pinched between my fingers. She released a soft moan that I swallowed greedily.

Her hands fisted my shirt, her hips rocked into mine, a sweet torture I savored. Swiftly, I dropped my hands to her thighs to raise her up, one leg forced to each side of my body. I reached down between us to tear at the obstructive attire we both wore. Her skirt had bunched when I lifted her, her undergarments now rags at our feet. My trousers fell to greet them even as my hips drove forward. She cried out.

"Fuck." I cursed into her ear, my hand raised to wrap behind her back and latch onto her shoulder.

Her nails found their way down my back over my shirt. I wanted to feel them on my skin. Feel her scratch them down my flesh as I took her. My growl with each score seemed to convey my desire. She scratched harder, shredding my shirt to leave trails down my spine. I could smell blood, faint notes I knew were mine, the stronger scent I knew as hers.

The realization only heightened my desire. My cock thrust harder within her, pulling out halfway before slamming back inside. The picture on the wall beside us fell, knocking over a vase that sat on the table below. It meant nothing. All I cared about at the moment was the impossibly tight channel that milked my need from me. The moans that grew loader every time I drove my length deeper. My name a chant on her breathless voice.

Her legs wrapped around my waist; my left hand free to tease her breast that was caught within my grasp. My right hand moved from her hair to her thigh as I dominated her body. Committing every inch to memory. I fucked her. I was not gentle. I did not hold back. Yet she begged me to continue every time my name slipped past her lips. I felt her tense, and knew she rode along the edge of her own climax.

"Not yet." I bit her bottom lip before releasing it.

This time, I knew what to expect when that velvety droplet appeared. Quickly I bit my own lip then kissed her, our blood mixed in our mouths sending us both over the edge. I growled deep in my chest, driving deep inside until I felt the last shutter of her orgasm subside.

My shaft twitched inside her, wetness running down my thigh as I held her there. She tried to unhook her legs, her assumption we were done bringing a laugh from my chest.

"That was only round one."

In two seconds, I had us in my room, Jenna on my bed beneath me. I rolled my hips to confirm for her that I remained solid inside her. Her back arched, a faint smile on her lips. She rolled me over onto my back. I could see it in her aura, the need to be in control here and now.

Her brown eyes turned red, and I knew mine must be a mixture of my own natures. We knew we did not have to fear harming one another. Jenna placed her palms on my chest, her hips rising and falling in a slow rhythm while her eyes slid from mine to my throat.

"Do it, Jenna. Feed from me."

She swallowed hard, lowering herself so her chest pressed against mine but never slowing her hips. I was losing my restraint, needed to fuck her hard, yet I was certain she knew that too. She licked the thick vein in my throat, sucked on my earlobe only to allow her teeth to scratch the skin when pulling back. When she sank her teeth into my vein, she began to move harder against me. Her hips rocked back and forth, my hand reaching between us to rub her clit.

Her moans sent vibrations through my body; my hips bucked up to meet her thrusts. I felt her walls constrict around my cock, the tremble in her muscles telling me she was near another orgasm. I bit her neck, the temptation too great as my hand wrapped around the back of her neck. She came harder than before, crying out into the night. I followed, filling her as I drank.

She rolled to the side, separating us for the first time since we had begun. My whole body protested, but it was the pain that I felt attempting to harm me that made me grab her arm and pull her to my side.

"Never took you for the cuddling type."

"No sense in you leaving when there is much more to do."

"Presumptuous of you, Mr. Castillo." She laughed.

"Yes, but I believe it is a quality you enjoy."

"Ass."

"You remain quite the lady, Jenna. Get some rest for now."

CHAPTER 20

~ HIM ~

A glass bottle shattered against the door behind the cowering man's head. He had entered thinking something had needed to be cleaned, instead he found his Master in a fit of rage.

"He was not to become attached to her. He becomes attached and he will seek for more answers than before. If he involves the elders with what he knows, or goes to see the others, then they might figure out what is going on. It is too soon."

He sent the servant away, then pulled the book from the stand and opened it. The prophecy foretold in blood had not changed, but with the prophet long dead, the writing could not change. Perhaps he should have kept him as a prisoner instead of killing him. His arrogance got the better of him.

There were only three now that could tell him if the prophecy remained. To ask them meant he would have to reveal part of his plan. They would want payment too. A heftier price than the last time, when they had told him where to find the prophet. No doubt they knew the prophet was dead. How could they not? He could send another in his place, but there was still the matter of payment.

Another idea formed. Two could die, to be eventually replaced, as long as one survived. One he could enslave this time. If he failed, or any found out what he did, he would be the one in a cell and tortured for eternity. He sat down. Another letter penned and slipped into an envelope with a black wax seal. A gravestone with wings in front of it pressed into the hot wax before it cooled. He rose from his seat, exited the room, and sought a servant.

"Deliver this immediately. No one else is to see it and you are to watch them burn it after they read it. Fail me and you will wish for death."

The young man dropped his eyes to the envelope, visibly paling when he saw where he had to go. Demons were never to be trusted. He knew he might not survive the journey or live long enough to watch them read the message. He also knew he could not refuse, or he would die right here and now. He nodded; the envelope tucked into his jacket pocket as he turned to go.

"Sacrifices are always necessary." He called out after the young man.

Returning to his study, fingers traced the words on the page. He would not fail. He had invested too much into this endeavor. Jenna was awake. She had yet to realize her full potential, but it was unlocked within her. It was just a matter of time now. Something he had plenty of, though he was not above speeding things along. Another note written, another servant sent to deliver it, meant that Marcus and Jenna's existence was about to become a lot more complicated. What was more interference when he had already ordered the deaths of two of the Fates?

CHAPTER 21
~ JENNA ~

I stretched out, my hand smoothing over cold sheets. My eyes opened to find Marcus was nowhere in sight. I flipped onto my back, recalling the night's activities. His taste lingered on my lips, the memory of what happened ushering a contented sigh from my lips. Marcus was the first person I had had sex with since Victor. With that my only experience, I had not expected to enjoy it quite as much as I had.

Part of me wanted to have him between my thighs again, and often. Getting up, I opened the door, knowing no one was in the hallway. I was naked, but I was not ashamed of it. Marcus would be the only one capable of sneaking up on me. I had finished dressing when I first heard the noise. Men were surrounding the house. Mortal men.

"Jenna, we have to leave."

"What's going on?"

"It's the church. Somehow, they discovered you were responsible for the massacre at the convent and that you are here."

"The church?"

My head whirled with the information. The church had a militia for what, monster hunting? Marcus pushed me toward the doors, turned me when we reached the bottom of the stairs, then through the passageway into the library underground.

"Marcus, what are you doing? We can't hide down here!"

"We aren't."

He moved to the table with the runes, placing his hands on the fabric, which shimmered with every hushed word he spoke. A blinding light filled the room, which was gone when the light faded away. We stood in a corridor painted in a soft blue, a wooden floor rested beneath our feet, and lights that I couldn't place lit the space from overhead.

"You need to leave. I knew you still had it. Destroyed my arse." A woman's stern voice broke the silence.

I turned to see a woman who looked to be in her forties with blonde hair and hazel eyes. She was heavier set, with skin so radiant that I knew it would be soft to the touch. Her hair was half clipped up, with the long locks flowing down her back. She was gorgeous. More than that, she held herself high. I could tell at once she was a fierce woman who did not back down from anything.

"Mrs. Thomas, I would not have come if it wasn't important. I am not here for myself, but for her. Besides, I received word that my debts were being settled."

"Settled? Do you really think anything you do can balance what you have done? The lives you took to gain power are forfeited forever. However, yes, we were informed a transaction was in the works we will have to honor. I did not, though, hear it was completed."

"It's not. This woman is the obligation I must fulfill. When she turned, she killed an entire convent full of nuns and some priests. Someone sent word that she was with me, and they showed up to take her. You know as well as I do, we can't allow her to be taken by them."

Mrs. Thomas sighed, turning. Marcus nodded for me to follow them. While we walked, I thought of what I had heard. Who had Marcus killed and for what power? And who was clearing his debt in return for helping me? I got the distinct feeling neither of them knew the answer.

"I will clear your access on a probationary status, Marcus. One step out of line and you will be immediately cast out. This time, no one will be able to get you reinstated with The Host."

"I require only one thing. To speak with the grand coven leader."

Mrs. Thomas stopped to look at him for a long moment before she pointed to a door on our left I hadn't noticed. Marcus took my hand and led me across the threshold without hesitation. Beyond the door was a cave. I had heard The Agora was a crossroads of sorts, but to see it surprised me. The cave had furnishings for one to live in comfortably enough. The thing calling my attention were the rows of shelves lined with all sorts of jars.

"What is it you seek, Mr. Castillo?"

"A talisman so I can walk in the daylight."

"That's no easy task. Though," A man not much older looking than Marcus looked my way. His white hair caught the candlelight and when our eyes met, I noted that his eyes were white as well. "With a drop of her blood, I can do it."

"Deal." Marcus pulled me to the man who was looking through his jars.

"Excuse me?" I yanked my hand away from him.

"Jenna, you need me alive, and this will help, so do it."

"You know, Mr. Castillo, if you hadn't welcomed that demonic power in, you would be able to walk in the daylight."

"Just do it." He held my hand out, the leader pricking the tip of my finger with a dagger. Several drops of blood dripped into a vial he held.

Pulling free again, I glared at Marcus and made my way back out of the room. The same door taking me instead to a garden full of fresh blooms. I slammed the door behind me, walking along a pathway of paver stones. Little fairies flit about from flower to flower, their wings glowing brightly. One flew near, allowing me to make out her features. Bigger eyes with pointy ears close to her head, her hair was red and short, with a thin body. She darted forward as if she was going to attack, but then suddenly went back to the others and they all scattered.

"They don't like what they are not familiar with." I turned to see Mrs. Thomas standing a few feet away. "Come, walk with me for a while. You can tell me how you came to be under the care of Mr. Castillo and anything else you care to share."

This woman appeared to be close to my mother's age, however, her presence reminded me more of my grandmother. We walked for a few minutes in silence, stopping when we came to a circular area with benches lining the edges and a fountain in the middle. The woman in the center was in the embrace of a man with large wings, a jug in her hands, overflowing with water that trickled down to the pool beneath their feet. Mrs. Thomas sat on one bench and patted beside her. Sitting there, we both stared at the statue. I took in every detail, feeling it was somehow familiar.

"They were lovers. Centuries ago, mortals did know of our world. Greed and fear made it necessary for us to exclude them over time. Believe it or not, but that is the true depiction of Salazar and Eve. The story has been quite slaughtered, saying Salazar was not the one for Eve, and she was made from a man. The truth is, Salazar used to tell her all the time that he wasn't whole until he met her. Adam was extremely jealous because he wanted Eve. He began to spread lies about Salazar, saying he had tricked Eve. Bad things began to happen around the village and

Adam placed all the blame at their feet. He told everyone they were being punished because Eve was under Salazar's enchantment. Now how the apple and the rest formed, I am not sure, but their story is one example of when our worlds began to split apart."

"What happened to them?"

"Adam's plan sadly did not work out for him. He made everyone fear Salazar and Eve. One day when she was out for a walk, some of the villagers captured her and took turns stabbing her. Salazar found her later when she didn't come home. No one really knows what happened to him. Adam said he saw him cradling her body and made a vow before disappearing that they would all pay one day. But we have to consider the source and that there hasn't been a single known act of vengeance. Many believe Salazar was so distraught that he shut himself away or worse."

"I can't imagine what he must have felt."

"Can't you? I can tell you are a vampire, turned not born. So, you had your own death, your own tragedy, your own loss."

"I know. I want my vengeance too for what was done to me but, I get to continue on. I am enraged. It boils deep within, always waiting to be released, but I have come to understand I can live. I have a purpose."

"I sense that too. If you ever decide you want to focus on that purpose, we could use your assistance here at The Agora. There are times we handle things for our guests. You would be in control of when and where you help. Keep it in mind when you free yourself from Marcus. He is not the man you seem to think he is. Do not trust him."

She patted my hand, rose, and left me there alone. I looked up, realizing the ceiling was painted to look like a sunny day, warmth of the sun shone brightly but it was not here. Witchcraft. I stared up at the painting, noticed after a while how the colors were changing into pink and orange hues. I didn't have to look to know Marcus was nearby. He moved to sit beside me, but when he went to take my hand, I pulled away.

"Ok. I understand you are upset."

"Upset? You forced me to give a drop of my blood. Would I have done so willingly? Most likely. You took the choice from me, though. Let us call that your first mistake and move on."

CHAPTER 22
~ MARCUS ~

She appeared more than merely upset. I didn't care. Everything had been acquired for us to proceed. I glanced down at the ring on my pinky. The gem glowed red once more, then faded. The talisman would allow me to walk in the day, but even more interesting, it might block the person who kept inflicting pain around Jenna. I would have to test that part later, when she was calm.

"Come on. We cannot stay here."

"You mean, you cannot."

"Listen, they attacked my home because of you. This is all happening because of you. So, stop being so spiteful and move."

I saw her shoulders slump a little. She knew I was right. Until I learned exactly what she was, and who was behind sending me to her, I was not letting her go. I had not survived so long by ignoring threats, and regardless of anything else, Jenna posed a threat.

I showed her the way to a shop where we were able to get some more suitable clothes and then led her through the front doors. They opened onto a busy street far from where we had begun. That was the beauty of The Agora, it existed everywhere and nowhere.

"Where are we?"

"The Americas."

"What?" She turned to meet my eyes.

"Relax. They won't find us here for quite some time and now that we know they are looking for you, we can be better prepared."

It was then that I saw her look at the blazing sun, then down to me in a panic. I chuckled, flashing the ring in front of her. A look crossed her face as she seemed to piece together the meaning.

"My blood did that?"

"Your blood, a butte load of elemental blessing, and payment. As long as I wear this, I can walk without worrying. Now let's go."

I led her through the streets to a carriage house near the outskirts of town. Those we passed watched us with interest. Even for a larger city by their standards, most were known and certainly all with status. I did not get a word out before the older gentleman was instructing his younger apprentice to gather his carriage. This was a place used to store or repair carriages for those around town. For over a decade, my own had been stored here. I saw the young man head to the back of the building, a large black cloth billowing out from the corner surrounded by a cloud of dust. I oversaw the preparations while Jenna stood outside, taking in her new surroundings. I had a place about thirty minutes outside of town, with enough land as to not deal with any neighbors. Of course, they would have to climb the eight-foot wall that surrounded the property first.

When everything was ready, I took the reins and extended my hand to her. She climbed aboard without a word and remained that way the entire ride to my estate. She was angrier than I thought. This would not do, not if I was to continue training her and learning more about what she was. When we arrived, the servants that lived there came out immediately.

"Benjamin, I presume. I trust everything has been maintained to my specifications?"

"Yes, Sir."

"Good. This is my companion, Miss Jenna Devereaux. See to it that our things are taken care of and then have tea brought to the study. Miss Devereaux and I need to talk."

"Please make sure our belongings are in separate rooms." She stated coldly as she stepped inside.

"Hell no, they will not."

I stormed in after her, gripping her arm tight, I led her into the study and slammed the door shut. I caged her between the door and my body. My cock rose in anticipation. The swollen length pressed into her as she tried to get away.

"Stop. You are acting like a child."

"A child? You forced me to give a drop of my blood. Took it without actually asking, then act like it is nothing."

"Nothing? Are you really so daft? You walked in the daylight the moment after your death. You blast me with some fucking energy after your blood damn near turns me savage. Then, on top of all that, your aura nearly fucking blinds me. Your blood is definitely not nothing, Jenna. You are not some ordinary turned vampire. You're not a shifter, either or a witch or fae of any kind I have known. So why don't you get a damn grip and realize you may be one of, if not the strongest fucking creature I have ever met. I am not sure if I should send you away or fuck you senseless and keep you."

"Well, I know what part of you thinks."

"Yeah, like your body disagrees?"

I could smell her arousal and damn if that wasn't making things more difficult. A clear head was needed to navigate the surrounding mess. I had to know just what she actually was, and I had one favor I knew I could call on to help. The debt I would owe later would be great, but there was no other option left.

"We are staying here until I can work something out. We will move when I say, and you will continue to train, learn, and test your limits so we know exactly what you are capable of. Am I clear?"

"Crystal, sir."

"Say that last part again."

Her pulse pounded, breathes rough as if she were ready to attack me at any moment. Her rage was glorious, always there, ready to explode.

"Fuck you, Marcus. I am not playing your games."

"Then hit me. I know you want to."

I stepped back, my stance ready for a fight. She did not disappoint. Faster than previous sessions, she threw a right hook, connecting with my jaw. Blood splattered across the desk a couple of feet away. Righting myself, I saw her smile in triumph a split second before she kicked her left foot square into my chest, sending me backwards into the liquor cabinet that sat against the wall. Wood splintered, decanters and glasses shattered across the floor. I stopped holding back. My demonic and vampire essences made me faster and stronger than most. A lesson she was about to learn.

My nails elongated; I slashed them down her back after landing a solid punch that spun her. Her shirt shredded, falling down her left shoulder to rest above her breast.

"I should have shredded more."

"You win, you can shred it all. I win, you tell me what got you exiled from The Agora. It's about time I know exactly who I am dealing with."

"Deal."

I rushed her, exchanging blow after blow, neither of us relenting. I began to wonder if I might actually lose when she stepped back in preparation for another strike. She thought instead of acted. I countered her attack, grabbing her by the leg she swung so boldly and throwing her against the desk. My hand clasped the back of her neck, pressing her face down while I slid my other hand down her back.

I grabbed the tattered fabric of her shirt, tearing it off her and letting my fingers run down her soft skin. She stilled beneath me, and I leaned over her.

"I will stop if you say so. I won't hurt you, well, not much."

Running my hand down her back, she didn't speak, didn't try to get away. I held onto the top of her pants and tore them until her glistening mound was revealed. I ran my fingers over the wet entrance, dipping two fingers in hard. While still holding her neck, I thrust them inside her. Hushed grunts morphed into soft whimpers that grew louder. I could feel her walls clenching, the wetness that began to slip down my hand. Needing to taste her, I dropped to my knees, tongue joining the rhythm of my fingers. I pulled them out to rub and pinch her clit until she exploded. I greedily devoured her until she stopped shaking.

Standing up, I freed myself, immediately driving into her. Papers fell from the desk as her hands reached up to grip the edge. I knew she could handle me, had handled me, without restraint. I pounded her, letting my anger out on the entire situation, and yet I could see her aura shimmer with need. She needed this as much as I did. I grinned, slowed my hips to hear a frustrated groan from her lips. She tried moving her hips, but I held her in place. Deliberately, I dragged my length inside her at a slow pace until the torture became too much. Ramming into her body, her tightness pulsed with her release and sent me over the edge. My hips not stopping until every drop was spent.

Marcus had someone bring a dress to the study, then closed the door and moved to the wall where the bar had been. He found an intact bottle and two glasses, pouring a healthy amount into each, handing me one on his way to sit in the chair behind the desk.

"Now, we will stay here while I make arrangements. When we leave, we will travel first to China, then Japan, then a Buddhist temple where I have some contacts. After we finish there, we will go to Russia, Germany, along with several other countries. I have been too lax in your training. You will learn from masters in multiple fighting styles, while also working on tapping into your own strength and abilities. We will find out exactly what you are capable of. After all, we have all the time in the world."

He seemed so pleased with himself, but he wasn't wrong. We were there only two weeks before we were off. Japan. China. Africa. London. Italy. Germany. Russia. Indonesia. Every place was a new lesson in the language, fighting styles, meditations, the clans, covens, packs, or families that resided in each.

I felt as though I looked down to slip on my dress in a shattered study to look up to a different world. How much had changed around us. Overpopulation. Cars. Planes. The digital age was upon us. Luckily, we adapted right along with it. The Agora's unit that had previously gone out on assignments had a cyber unit tasked with searching for and destroying any evidence of our world.

The world was dangerous for us now, in many ways. There were governmental groups that knew enough to investigate our existence, as well as fringe groups within the mortals, and of course those hungry for the gifts we possessed. Our most lethal enemy, the church. They had kept records from the time when our worlds were not so separate. They wished to eradicate all of us who were not mortal.

Keeping your guard always up, though, is impossible, even for us. Which is why I am now shackled to a wall in an underground prison beneath the most holy of places for the Catholic church.

"The source was right again. This time she didn't get away, though. It took us four times the number of tranquilizers to subdue her. We lost ten men in the process as well."

"Come closer and I will make it eleven." My head felt heavy, but that was lifting quickly. I took a step forward, using all my strength not to stumble, the fear in their eyes as they stepped back my reward.

"We have been hoping to capture you for centuries, Miss Devereaux. Ever since the night you slaughtered forty nuns and several priests. Since then, you have killed many more whenever we attempted to remove your filth from this earth."

"Yet you kept coming. Am I so high on your most wanted list? I guess I should have killed more so you would get the hint. Pity. Or...Were you all just that hard up? Nothing else to occupy your time? You know there is porn on the computers now, right? Maybe take in a movie? A vacation?"

"Not just ours, but it would seem someone in your own

society as well. We have received letter after letter, then emails, phone calls, all untraceable, telling us where to find you and your companion. Pity he wasn't there when we came by."

"If he was, you would have all died."

"No, I fear if he had, some of us would have suffered a far worse fate than death."

"Like he would try to turn any of you assholes."

"You really don't know, do you? Your companion set up his own network a long time ago, selling us off to be farmed for our blood and, later, our organs. Hearts for werewolves or witches. Same with most every other body part. According to our records, it started as a debt he owed for a special ring he had forged. This became his own empire. He does not discriminate either. Men, women, children, infants, all available to the highest bidder."

A switch flipped inside my mind; Marcus lost his privileges at The Agora not long after he got them back. I had even spoken to several generations since, to see if I could learn why, but none would give a reason. They didn't care a lot about a death here or there, but to harvest and sell mortals was crossing the line. If they allowed him access, it would be like saying it was ok and that could cause complications with others. I suppose even The Host had his limits of what he would tolerate.

When I got out, I would confront Marcus and get him to shut it down. I wondered though if he would do it for me. I cared for Marcus, and I believed he cared for me, but neither of us ever brought up bonding to the other. A sword puncturing my abdomen brought me back to reality.

"Let her bleed out a bit to keep her weak. You will have to keep stabbing her when she heals to drain enough blood. Just make sure not to kill her. We need information from her about the mysterious benefactor. They seem to know too much about us, so after we are through with her, we need to close that gap."

Fuck. Healing or not, it hurt. They barely waited for the

wound to heal before they stabbed again. Apparently, they were impatient because as soon as the one who seemed to be in charge left, the three that remained decided to expedite the process. Cuts along my arms and legs healed more slowly. They stopped stabbing my gut when they realized how much I had already lost. One moved close, dagger slicing along my collarbone.

"Bitch. That is for my friends that you killed."

"They tasted like shit."

"You fucking cunt!" He stabbed into my chest, piercing my heart.

"And I thought priests were pussies."

"Fuck, he's going to be pissed. Fuck. You better hope that she makes it somehow."

"I don't care if she dies. What's he going to do? Not like she needs a heart, anyway. Her boyfriend has just been using her too, to learn who is behind the black seal. Capturing a couple of his men proved as much."

My head slumped, the chains the only thing keeping me from falling onto the floor. I had confided in Marcus about the voice, and he admitted that until he had the ring, whenever he would think of touching me, he would get an intense pain through his head. Seemed the ring made with my blood did more than allow him to walk in the sun.

Recently, the voice had become more insistent. Commanding me to come to them, saying how I could not avoid my destiny. Even my dreams had become a way for him to communicate, but even there I could not see who he was. A shadow, always out of reach with words that offered no comfort.

"I suppose this may be one way to escape him." Blood fell from my lips when I coughed.

I wasn't going to die from this, but I would end up unconscious for as long as my body took to heal, which with no blood could be a very long time. What they might decide to do with me in the meantime; I didn't know. I certainly didn't see any of them feeding me.

Consciousness fading away, I thought I heard screams mix with the melody of the bells overhead as I surrendered to the darkness. What beautiful sounds the Vatican had.

I walked right through the front gates with a tour group. I am not sure if they didn't expect me to be so bold or if they thought I wouldn't come at all. The problem was, they had something of mine. Something I wanted back.

When the group entered a long corridor, I made my exit. An associate got me the intel I needed to find my way into the lower levels. I was certain that was where they would keep her. Part of me said to cut my losses and move on. There was no way for me to know what awaited me below. The other part had grown fond of her and wasn't ready to let her go. I needed her to find out what game was being played, but I wasn't sure anymore if that was the strongest reason. I wanted her around. Even when her attitude got to me, I wanted to have her near.

"Fucking hell. When did I become so pathetic? I am really charging into the Vatican to save one woman. Killing anyone who tries to stop me and putting myself at the top of their list for her. I really owe the fucker that put us in each other's lives."

Making my way through the first set of doors with the counterfeit key card, I found two guards standing by the next entryway. I turned the corner immediately, babbling and pretending not to understand their questions.

"I'm sorry. I think I am lost. I can't find the group I was with. When I stopped to look at the statues, they were gone. What? I am sorry, but I don't understand you."

I moved closer and looked around as if in awe while speaking until I was close enough. My hands flew up to either side of the first guard's head. A quick twist with a popping sound took care of him. The other pulled a pistol out, the muffled shot landing somewhere in the wall behind me. I grabbed his arm, bringing my elbow down to break it before I grabbed his head to snap his neck. I dragged both bodies to a corner and haphazardly pulled the window curtains to cover most of them.

Entering the door they had guarded, I found it was an elevator that required a key to go to the sub-levels. Going back to search them, I found the key and quickly returned. Standing in the small space, I looked for any cameras, but found none that I could see. Still, I prepared for an ambush as soon as the doors opened again.

With a quiet ding, they opened to a dimly lit hallway. I smelled her blood the second I stepped off. I ran down the hall in her direction. Men that got in my path ended up on the floor, with either their throats or hearts ripped out or their head torn completely off. My rage only grew the stronger her scent became.

In the final room, I found three men holding daggers. Behind them lay a bloody sword on the ground. My rage filled eyes turned black as I took in the back wall. Jenna was slumped over with arms outstretched in chains. Her clothes were soaked in blood, a crimson puddle at her feet.

I scarcely recall what happened. My demonic nature took over, which had only ever occurred once before. Two of the men dropped to their knees in prayer. I focused on both and made them feel their guilt a thousand times over. The daggers they held were turned inward, piercing their own hearts even as they begged for mercy. The last felt no remorse for anything. Had a demon gotten to him before the church, he would have been convinced to be a serial killer. His soul was a delightful sight, but today, he would still die.

When he raised his dagger to fight me, I walked up to him. I moved behind before he could land a blow and punched his back to paralyze him. Dragging him over to her, I yanked the chains from the wall, catching her before she hit the ground. Placing her on her back, I moved her hair from her face and made sure her mouth was open. Grabbing the man, I ignored his curses. Using my nail, I slit his throat over her mouth. His blood fell, splattering her face and neck, droplets glistening in her hair like sapphires. I held him there until I no longer heard his heartbeat, then tossed him aside.

Cradling Jenna in my arms, I let out a ragged breath when her eyes fluttered open. I could feel her strength returning quickly. As she focused on me, I saw a flash of red.

"You done playing around? How about we get out of here?"

She wiped her mouth, sat up quickly, but then leaned on me to stand. Getting her bearings, she kept looking at me but didn't say a word.

"Okay, Jenna. This is getting fucking weird. You are never without something to say or yell at me for."

"Tell me it isn't true."

"Tell you what isn't true."

"Cut the act, Marcus."

"What did they tell you?"

"That you have been taking mortals to use as animals for milking, basically. Harvesting their blood, and their bodies to sell off."

"Mortals do it to animals all the time. Why should they be above it? Besides, it helps our world not just survive, but to thrive.

I won't feel guilty about it, Jenna. I also won't stop, so don't ask. That's why I never told you about it."

"I can't believe you would victimize so many innocent people."

"Jenna, this really isn't the time or the place for this conversation. Besides, I told you centuries ago. I am a monster. It's who I have always been."

"And me? You've just been using me, too?"

"Yes." One word said quickly in response.

"Really? Nothing from our time together has meant anything to you?"

"What do you want me to say? That I care for you? I do. But that doesn't change the fact that I have and will continue to use you."

"You really are an asshole, Marcus. If I ever see you again, I will kill you. For your sake, I hope you shut down your side business."

Walking past me, she had one last surprise. She tore the ring from my finger, squeezing it in her palm. Her eyes changed to that blinding white light. When it faded, my ring was broken on the ground, and she was already heading down the hallway toward the elevator.

I could have run after her. Called out to her. Tried to make it up to her, get her to see things my way. I couldn't. She deserved the truth after all these years. So, I watched her go until I couldn't see her and when she was gone from my sight; I felt something inside break.

CHAPTER 25

~ JENNA ~

When I exited the elevator, two men were examining the bodies off in a corner. They turned when they heard the doors open and came charging at me. I took my outrage out on them. One pulled a gun and when he pointed it at me, I grabbed his wrist and spun to avoid the bullet grazing by my head to sink my fangs into his throat.

A couple of deep gulps was all I could savor when a bullet ripped through my right shoulder into the man's chest. I turned to see the other guard shaking with the pistol in his hands. Pain radiated out from the wound, but did not stop me from leaping onto him. I sunk my fangs deep, drinking hungrily to sate my thirst and restore my strength.

Another shot rang out, narrowly missing me from the doorway. I cut my eyes to the left to see another guard standing there, ready to fire. Footsteps sounded from behind him, reminding me that I needed to get out fast. Before he could pull the trigger, I leapt through the window, small cuts from the sharp glass healing even as I spun and landed on my feet below.

I didn't look back. Screams followed me out of the shattered window, confirming that Marcus had entered the room. Hundreds of years and I never really knew him. He never really knew me either if he thought I would ever be ok with using innocents as cattle.

I ran from the Vatican, grabbing a cell phone from a woman yelling at the person on the other end about being late. I could hear her confused curses when her phone vanished from her hand. Hanging up, I dialed. Only two rings sounded before I heard the voice on the other end.

"I had a feeling you would be calling. Perfect timing too."

"One day you will have to tell me how you do that."

"We all have our secrets, Jenna. Make a right at the next corner, then go through the black door at the end of the block. We will see you soon."

She hung up without saying anything else, not that I really expected her to. Joanna was always that way. When the conversation was over, she was gone whether or not you agreed. I followed her instructions, walking through the door and into The Agora.

Joanna stood there waiting for me, with a young blonde woman next to her. Given the resemblance, I knew exactly who she was, even if my eyes could not believe it. Had it really been so long since I had snuck away to come here?

"Joanna. Carissa. I am just realizing that it's been too many years since I have been here."

"Well, not like you could always come. Though our doors are always open to you. Our ancestor said that you were special and that you might need us."

"I suppose not, and I have found nothing recently that I needed help with. Same appears to be true for you. I don't believe I've had a request for any favors in about five years."

"But that's not why you've come to us now, is it?" Joanna stepped aside and extended her arm.

We walked together to her office; Carissa closed the door that disappeared. I had already seen this little trick. I assumed it was a mix of security for them and to keep control over any meetings. Quite the leverage tactic when the other party was trapped.

"So..." she handed me a glass of bourbon and I saw Carissa's eyebrows furrow.

"Something wrong?"

"She has been negligent in her studies. I think she was under the impression you only drank blood."

"Well, vampires don't have to eat or drink anything else. We even have reflections and many of us love garlic. With training, some can learn to walk in the sun."

"I know all that. I was just surprised you liked that stuff."

Joanna and I both laughed. I sipped the amber liquor, seating myself in the chair by the desk.

"I won't be going back to Marcus. I would like to make our previous agreement more permanent."

"What agreement?" Carissa stepped forward.

"I apologize. Carissa is beginning to take on more responsibility here, but keeps forgetting how much there is to learn."

"She's eager and young. She'll get it, eventually."

"I am standing right here."

"We know, dear. I told Jenna years ago that if she ever needed it, we would set her up with a place to live and a document trail separate from Marcus. I knew that the need would likely arise at some point. The agreement is in her file."

"I have a file?"

"Figuratively speaking. Yes. Everyone does."

"Too bad the files don't know everything." I got up to refill my glass.

"We have been over that before, Jenna. You are the only person, that I've checked at least, whose file does not state your species."

"I really won that lottery that night. Makes no difference now. I'm not sure if that little file of yours is up to date or not, but I have learned a hell of a lot over the years."

"Do you really have to curse?"

"No, but then again, why the fuck not?"

Joanna rolled her eyes and got up. Handing a key to me, she looked at Carissa. They didn't speak, but I felt certain they were talking. The Thomas family had become a mystery to me over the years. Something about them just not adding up. They weren't witches or fae of any kind, nor were they vampires or shifters. I wondered if they got their abilities from The Host. One day, I really wanted to meet him.

CHAPTER 26

~ HIM ~

The woman knocked lightly on the door as if she hoped he would not hear it. He liked that they all fear him. He found it amusing and convenient since he continuously found their news disappointing. The demons had yet to complete their task, despite having over a century. His request to have the Fates killed has become something of a competition for them now.

Even their ruler had heard of the competition but, like most, was in the dark as to who had made the request. All that they knew was one must be kept alive. He really didn't care which one it was.

"Come in."

"Sir, we received word about the woman. She has separated from Marcus. She is at The Agora with the Thomas family. The source stated she has told them she has put off her purpose for too long. She plans to aid them in exchange for their assistance, and to pass the time until she solidifies her own network."

"About bloody time." He couldn't stop the laugh that

bellowed out. She was no longer with Marcus, so now if he needed to be dealt with, he could do so easily.

"Let me know where she settles. Her nature is too restless to remain there. She will feel stifled. I want to know the second her residence changes. Do I make myself clear?"

"Yes, Sir."

She scurried out of the room like a mouse who just spotted a cat ready to pounce. Another lost soul that was always too timid for life.

"You will have your new home. Your freedom for a time. A short time, but my patience has run out. We will be seeing each other soon, my sweet Jenna."

CHAPTER 27
~ JENNA ~

It didn't take long for Joanna to get me set up. Holdings that Marcus had helped set up were stripped clean, so he could access nothing of mine. I set up a new contact through The Agora for financial matters, as well as a schedule for new identities, fake wills, and the like, so all the paperwork was always in order.

"You know you are still not safe, Jenna."

"I know. I also know their tactics. Let those priests come again. If I must, I will kill them all. Maybe they will learn to leave me alone. What happened was so long ago, the history books don't mention it. I had just been reborn, and the thirst was all-consuming. To think that I live with the memory of everyone in the convent should be enough."

"The church has always held a grudge."

"If only they knew the truth about most of their stories and their..."

A knock on the door cut me off. A man stood in the doorway with a clipboard. I walked over, a practiced amiable smile on my lips.

"Ms. Devroo? Deveroo?"

"Devereaux." I gave a soft laugh while taking the clipboard.

"We got a lot a stuff to bring up. You have a larger elevator?"

"Yes, there is one down the hall to your left when you leave. Here is the key."

He took the key with obvious relief. When he was gone, I turned back to Joanna.

"Tell me again why one of the witches couldn't just furnish the place for me."

"If you are going to live here for a while, you need to be seen as somewhat normal."

"Normal is overrated." I walked past her to unpack a few of the boxes we brought with us.

I poured a glass of bourbon, raising my brow to her only to see her quickly shake her head and her hand. She had never really been one to drink often. To look at us now, no mortal would believe that our first meeting had been when she was six years old. She looked like she could be my mother.

We stood around the island in the kitchen, neither saying a word. Joanna was the one who broke the silence with a question I knew she had been considering.

"What if Marcus comes back? Will you really kill him?"

"Most likely. He would have to say the right words quickly for me not to."

"Do you think you really can kill him?"

"Yes. In our training, I've learned most of what I am capable of. It's been enough to scare every trainer I have had, even Marcus. With the exception of blood loss, I have none of the vampire weaknesses. I am stronger than turned vampires twice my age, faster too. Starvation doesn't affect me as quickly either. I have been able to walk in the sun since day one."

"That is your vampire essence. What about the other attributes?"

"My eyes don't simply turn red, but can go black, white, or a strange swirl of all three. The white I can now control to blast a blinding flash. The black seems to sink those that stare into an abyss. With both, I feel this sensation or weight of their lives. There is also this ability to send out a shockwave, to push anyone or anything away."

"No, dear. That's just your sparkling personality."

"Bitch." I laughed while refilling my glass and filling one for her. "Don't make me drink alone."

"One."

"Two. Three. I can count too."

"You are a woman I will never understand. You can be so kind one minute and so deadly the next. Especially if someone innocent is hurt. Are you ever going to tell me what happened all those years ago? Other than what we pieced together, no one has been able to compile all the details."

"They don't need to. Talking about it won't change anything. I told your ancestors all they needed to know with their promise that if Victor ever showed on their radar, they would tell me and only me."

"Did it help when he finally did?"

"No. He died too quickly. The coward saw me and Marcus and ran out into the fucking sun, then jumped off the thirty-story building we were in. He cheated me out of my revenge. He lost too much blood and decimated so much of his body. His face was so calm when he ran. There wasn't any fear. I can't forget it."

"Some believe you are lucky not to have killed him. He was sired by one of the remaining elders."

"Screw them. They only ever come out of hiding when they feel they have been disrespected."

She sipped her drink while eyeing me over the rim. I think she knew that even if I had known, I still would have killed him.

The movers came back and forth carrying a couple of couches, tables, chairs, a desk, bed, and mirrors. They unwrapped and set everything out, then took all the garbage with them.

While they worked, we kept the conversation light. Using names and avoiding species or clan references, she caught me up on most of what had been happening at The Agora. I recalled the first time I had been there, when the lights overhead turned out to be fairies. There were always so many of them around.

Joanna recounted a story of when electricity was first installed, and the fairies no longer helped the spells light the place. Many were upset, so they expanded the garden to give them more room to roam. That statue remained in the center. I had been in the garden on many occasions, sitting by the statue had become my sanctuary.

For me, life was ordinary. I could walk through my bedroom or bathroom door to enter The Agora. The few people I passed in the hallway or elevator of my building believed I simply worked from home. Another cover they set up for me. A job with payments and taxes and work even done in my name for some company.

I didn't even know the name of the place I allegedly worked for, even though I was told too many times. I had taken to fulfilling contracts through The Agora often, while also getting a Private Investigator license. This was a cover I liked. If ever I was caught anywhere, I simply told them I was working for a client. Privacy laws kept me from having to say more unless they got a warrant. By then, the lie was worked up with substance to pass any inquiries.

In doing jobs for them, I began to actually find others in need of help. I even worked with others from my world, which became beneficial. I now had connections with several covens, werewolf packs, and a couple of vampires. The vampire race seemed to have decided that I was an outcast. One not welcome within the inner sanctum.

I was not sure if this was because of what I was, an unknown, or a parting gift from Marcus. I kept tabs on him. I told myself it was because I wanted to avoid him, or make sure he was not doing worse things. Deep down, I knew that was a lie. Part of me cared for him. A few times I thought I had felt him near, my breath would catch, and I would seek him out. Every time, there was no one.

Today has been that way. Last night I had met with Carissa. As much as she was trying to be in charge, that girl needed a backbone. I had what I needed, so I walked out before she was done. She sat there calling after me with what sounded like confusion in her voice. I imagine I was once that way, but I don't wish her a traumatic event to toughen her up.

Perhaps that is why I find myself counseling her more as time goes on. She is in her early twenties, for today that is very young. She is, however, shaking things up a bit as well. She has asked that I investigate a matter mostly affecting the mortals in the slums. I know why she was reluctant to ask. There is the possibility that Marcus may be involved in the disappearances and deaths that have been taking place.

"Marcus, please tell me you have cleaned up your act. If not for me, then for yourself."

The day I moved in, Joanna had asked if I could kill Marcus. I immediately went into the technical aspect; she asked again days later, and I caught what she really meant. Physically, I knew I could win against him. The concern is whether I would be able to bring myself to do it. If he is behind this, I don't see what choice I have.

Standing up, I put my glass in the sink, then the liquor bottle back on the shelf. I didn't even succeed in getting a buzz with the special bourbon. I was not in the mood to drink. I considered going to a club and losing myself in someone. Man or woman made no difference to me anymore. Marcus saw to my education in all ways pleasure could be found. Thinking of the past, even that distraction lost its temptation.

"Fuck."

I walked toward the bathroom, intent on soaking in the tub. Passing the large mirror that ran almost the entire height of the wall, I paused, taking a couple of steps back. Turning to look at my reflection, another stood slightly blurred behind me.

"Jenna, my dear sweet Jenna. It is time. The games are over."

"You. Who the hell are you? What do you want? You have taunted me for centuries. How about you grow a set and come get me already?"

"That is rich coming from you. You have lived your entire life without ever being true to yourself until recently. However, you still don't know. I have the answers you seek. I am the only one that can answer them. All I ask is that you listen."

"You know what, jackass? You're welcome anytime."

"However dismissive, thank you."

Words that should be pleasant made me think of all the stories when a mortal signed their life away. The demon thanking them for their unknowing sacrifice. They never seemed to know what the cost really was.

As I watched now, I felt a wave of nausea wash over me, my ears picking up a hum which started off quietly. Before my eyes, he stepped from the mirror. He wore black boots, black jeans, with a black button-up shirt. Only a couple buttons were undone, revealing the very top of his chest, but it was the black hair and striking blue eyes that were almost too pale that held my focus. He was tall, thin, but muscular. Face to face with him, I was at once very thankful I had resisted his call. Every nerve in my body screamed that he would change my life in ways I could not imagine.

"Relax, Jenna. Sit. If I wanted to kill you or even hurt you, you would have died ages ago."

"Who are you?"

"My name is not important. What I have to say, well that is very important, so sit. I insist."

I wanted to bite back, but I was at a loss for words. So, I did as he said. I sat on the dark grey couch without ever taking my eyes off of him. He moved to the black leather chair to my right, legs crossed casually as he leaned back.

"I knew your mother. You look a little like her. I met her just before she got pregnant with you. She wasn't supposed to have you, or any child. That was her fate. I, shall we say, intervened. I was looking for a special soul that would be allowed to carry another very special soul. One I could assist further with."

"You're my father?" My voice was so loud that it startled me. If it surprised him, he didn't show it. Instead, he laughed.

"No, I did not sleep with your mother. I did help redirect you to her, and made sure you were not entirely defenseless. See, I have a considerable pull over death. That can come in handy when negotiating favors. All you really need to know is that you were never mortal. You were, well are, the Angel of Death."

"A Grim Reaper? You're saying *I* am a Grim Reaper?"

"No. Grim Reapers are purgatory souls forced to help see off the dead as punishment, or to help them find their own way to forgiving themselves or wallowing further in their guilt. Eventually, they end up being judged and their souls move along. We don't move along. There is no need to wait for a specific time of death. We can go to anyone and pass judgment. There is a lot of energy involved and, as you have found out, that can be used as a weapon."

"So, you're an Angel of Death too. How many of us are there? How did I become one?"

"Two."

"Excuse me?"

"I was the first and only until I assisted in your rebirth."

"You were involved with Victor?" My hand was on his throat instantly, nails pressed into his skin, but he only looked up at me with ease.

"Not that rebirth, Jenna. When your essence was reborn. As you can imagine, since I was the only one, I needed to help. The scent of your blood to a vampire is unknown. I have not walked among them for a very long time. I suppose it was bound to happen that some manner of creature would come across you and be too tempted to continue on his way. You did not know it, but you had been around several beings before. They lingered, curious to see if you would do anything. Of course, you never did. A few I had dispatched to avoid them taking or harming you. You see, I have always watched over you."

"That's just creepy. So why now? Why, after all these years, did you come here? Why call to me but never show up?" I removed my hand from his throat, the tips of my nails brought to my mouth. His blood tasted similar to mine. The scent of it held the same notes I could never place.

"I wanted to test you. Then I wanted you to learn. I saw how stubborn you could be. I thought it would be better if you realized how unique you are. That way, what I have to tell you would be easier for you to accept."

I moved away to pour some of the bourbon into two glasses. Coming back, I handed one to him without a word. He took the glass, sipping it slowly with a smirk curling one side of his lips. Watching him over the rim of my glass, I felt it. There was a connection here, the final piece of the puzzle within my grasp. I knew whatever he had to say would once more change my life. Hopefully, for the last time.

I didn't want to stay in my seat. My reaction to her was very strong. I purposefully sat in the chair instead of next to her. I knew I would reach out to touch her if I did. This time, it had worked. I could see her, smell her perfume when she came near, the softness of her palm when it pressed into my throat.

"Jenna, to an extent, I will always give you the time you need. I do have my limits, though."

"Let me guess. You're not a nice guy."

"No, I'm not. I never have been. Then again, you wouldn't want me to be nice."

She didn't reply, instead another sip of bourbon passed her lips.

"You said you dispatched people around me. You killed them or had them killed?"

"Does it matter?"

"Yes. I want to know what kind of psycho I am dealing with."

"Most I had brought to me, and I killed them myself. Some I killed slowly when they made it clear they had wanted to do the same to you. Now, let me tell you a story about a mortal woman who wanted a child."

She sat back on the couch, listening. Even after her glass ran dry, she did not get up. I told her how I needed someone who had a pure intention and love to have a child. I summarized how I found her mother, the deal we made, that she would have her daughter, but how one day, I would come for her. I assured her it would not be until years after she was an adult.

"I think that is why when you neared maturity, she began to keep you away from most. When you reached your twenties, I believe she thought I might not come for you. Explains why she finally let you out to court suitors. That... Well, that actually had me making some arrangements of my own when Victor happened to find you. You lost control when you found him. You wanted him dead for everything you had done."

"The asshole walked right out and jumped off the building rooftop."

"I know. I was watching. I also could sense his judgment. He saw what you were thinking about. All the guilt you laid at his feet. Those faces screaming, crying, begging, and your hatred for having killed them. Your desire for his death. He only jumped because of you. You made his last moments hell, and he struggled against it, knew he was going to die, and was powerless to stop you."

I saw the smile that spread across her lips. I wasn't lying to her. Lies were pointless. A little white lie would never leave my tongue. The last time it happened was well before the mortals wrote their bible. Events always shape us into someone new, one way or another.

"Why won't you tell me your name?"

"I will. Just not yet."

"Whatever. So, you helped my mother and father have me. Brought my essence, my soul, or energy from wherever it was to be reincarnated. Then you kept tabs on me. Watched over me. Killed people for me. Called out to me for centuries. Yet you waited until now to actually talk to me. See, something in your story doesn't add up, Jack. Why should I trust you?"

"You shouldn't. Know that I won't lie to you though. I don't need to."

"So, what exactly am I?"

"You are part vampire and part angel of death."

"Why bring back my soul?"

"Your soul means a great deal to a lot of people, myself included."

"Ambiguous much?"

"I am having someone brought to me that will tell you more about that. I think it'd be best coming from her."

"What do you want from me?"

There was the question I was waiting for. A smile grew across my face, leaning back, my elbows rested on the armrest while my hands gestured wide with a shrug of my shoulders.

"You, of course. I want you."

I nearly choked, despite the dryness of my throat. My mind had been imagining a million scenarios in response to that particular question. The boldness and simplicity of his response managed to set me off track.

"Me. Just me. Just like that. What the hell is that supposed to mean? You want to use me? Kill me? Take my blood? You're going to have to be a little more specific."

"You do have balls, Jenna."

"Yes, I know. Don't be jealous because mine are bigger, higher, and I don't have to think with them. Though they have been known to drop others IQ several points."

"It's nice to know that some things will never change, no matter what. You have always been headstrong and feisty."

"I get the feeling that this rebirth has you under the impression I am someone else. Despite any similarities you might see, I am not whoever this person was. I don't recall any other life other than my own and the one I have been living has, at times, been more like a nightmare."

"You will. It won't be long now. I promise you that."

He got up and came over to me, a business card between his fingers. I took it, looking for a name, but there was only a phone number below a pair of wings. My fingers traced the embossed image in silence.

"When you are complete, yours will reveal themselves. Black as those of the raven like mine. I am sure you have felt them even if you haven't seen them. Your willpower is so beautifully strong."

"Wings? I have wings? What are you…"

I looked up to see him with large black wings spread behind him. They were huge, knocking the side table against the wall as he stretched them wide. My throat closed, an ache in my back growing, then they were gone and so was he.

It took several minutes for me to regain my composure. I burst through the door to my bedroom only to enter the hallway of The Agora. A man, the head coven leader that I had seen before, stood there. His white hair was loose around his face, near white eyes looked me up and down as his jaw tightened and a single word ground out.

"No."

She was shaking, refusing her normal bourbon for a glass of water. If that was not enough to raise alarm, she was demanding to see the Host and the coven leader that had brought her to the office.

I still haven't figured out what was said between them, but he appeared pissed off while she seemed confused. In the time I have known Jenna Devereaux, she has never been confused. I glanced at my mother, who seemed as concerned as I was.

"Jenna, what is going on? We can't help you if you don't talk to us."

"Let me see your boss. He's supposed to be extremely powerful, right? He knows how to suppress what we are, which means he has to have some idea what that is. I finally got answers, but got a shitload of more questions."

"What are you talking about? What happened? Was it Marcus?"

"I don't know. He wouldn't give me his name. He had wings, Carissa. Fucking wings."

I exchanged another look with my mother.

"Jenna, angels have wings. Some elder vampires also have wings when they shift forms. There are even dragons," Joanna's words fell off when Jenna cut in.

"Yeah, like the Angel of fucking Death."

"Jenna, you have to be mistaken. There was someone who took up that role, but he's been gone for a very long time."

"He mentioned that."

"Ok. Ok. Wait. Let's say he's back. What does he have to do with you?"

"Apparently, he and I are one or some shit."

It was then I realized why she was shaking. I had thought she was traumatized. I wish I had been right. Instead, she was pissed.

"What exactly do you mean by that?" My mother chimed in.

"He used his essence or power to reincarnate my... what you call, soul."

She stood from the chair by the desk to look out the window I had put in. It didn't really exist, but it did show what was going on wherever you wanted to see within the site. Right now, it was looking into the garden. The statue in the center framed perfectly in view. She always made a point of sitting there on the bench during each visit. I would take her there now, but I didn't want anyone to hear us.

"Let me get this straight. Death brought you back by merging with you. So that would make you also Death. This is why you were so unique that no one could identify it! I mean, there's only one Death."

Jenna held up two fingers.

"Ok, yes, now I suppose that is true. But why? Who are you supposed to be?"

"He said someone else will tell me. They are being brought to him and when I know I will be complete and have big ass black wings like him."

"That's why you want to talk to him. To see if he can answer those questions without waiting for Death?"

"Yes. I also want to know how to kill or trap him in case it comes to that."

"You can't kill Death. I mean, we all thought he was gone, but only in the sense that he was in a state of hibernation or something. No one would dare to think he was dead, some may have hoped, but there are certain things that just are. Death is one of them."

"Everything can be killed. I learned that much in my studies, Carissa."

"Oh really, and how many have succeeded in killing you? Hell, how many have even come close?"

"Only a couple."

"And what happened to them?"

"They are all dead. It doesn't change things. I need to see him. I don't care if he never sees anyone. He has to see me. Please. I am tired of others trying to use or control me. He has been watching me my entire life. Your boss has to know something about it."

"I wish I could help you, Jenna. The answer is no."

CHAPTER 32
~ JENNA ~

I understood, but it didn't change the fury I felt growing inside. Every time I felt like I had my life on track, someone appeared out of the shadows, knowing more about me than I did. In all my training sessions, my meditations, my own rampant imagination, I never considered Death would end up on my doorstep. Or, looking glass may be a better description.

Instinct swore he knew the me I was before. Whoever I was, I had certainly gotten his attention. I left Carissa's office in favor of the garden. I sat at the first bench I saw, my eyes studying the fairies that went from one bud to another. They maintained the health of all the blooms. It wasn't a job to them. They enjoyed the task.

Joanna had told me she worried once they were overworked, so she asked a witch to assist. The fairies cut all the flowers touched by the spell down to the ground. She got the message loud and clear.

The fairies used to live in a beautiful forest. Humans had cut it down, paved the ground, and built buildings that kissed the sky. They were given refuge here. They can come and go as they please, but this is their home now. As more and more of the world's nature is lost, this place becomes their sanctuary. I have wondered if humans knowing would make a difference. Sadly, I don't think it would.

"Is it safe to approach?"

"Hey, Joanna."

"Jenna, I know you are disappointed. I promise, if I thought it would help, I would let you see him. He can't help you. I can't think of anyone that can."

"Apparently Jack knows someone."

"Jack?"

"Jack Ass, aka Death."

"Why don't we talk about something else? I know Carissa gave you information on the disappearances. Did you have any time to look into that before you were visited?"

"Joanna, you make it sound like Scrooge and the ghosts. Visited." I scoffed. "I put some feelers out on some of the names. Many came back quickly with ties to local gangs, drugs, trafficking, money laundering, etc. One woman that she gave me isn't missing. She took off to get away from her pimp with her kid. From my understanding, she went home. The rest will take more time. There is a small three block area they all seem to have in common. I will check it out tonight. I need something to get my mind off this shit."

"To look at you, anyone would think what a gorgeous woman you are. To talk to you, they would think a sailor has possessed your body."

"If there is one trying, he will have to fucking wait. I have enough fighting for control as it is."

CHAPTER 33

~ JENNA ~

The club was packed. A line of people stretched around the corner, waiting to get in. Wearing a slinky red dress, I barely had to use my persuasive abilities to get the bouncer to usher me through. Many of those in line would never be allowed in. Mortals that had found out there was a club here, or saw the entrance, stood in line, thinking they had found the best new place in town.

They would be sent home, disappointed and without the knowledge of how close they had come to the things that scare them in the night. Humanity had taken a different path. If they learned about us now, I had no doubt it would end in bloodshed.

I wondered what life was like before the downfall. The mortal humans and our world surviving as one. Those times must have been pleasant. Some areas would have had their quarrels, but it wouldn't have grown into what it is now.

Who was I kidding? Eventually, we would have ended up in this exact place. Greed. Jealousy. These were not emotions limited to their kind. Add in the abilities many of us had, and this was inevitable.

A glance around the club confirms that. While for many, this is just a night out, without fear of discovery, for others, this is a place to see who is around. A place to handle things they don't wish to handle anywhere else, or to satisfy desires that can only be found here. As long as no one dies, anything goes. It's the club's way of not getting their hands dirty. This is also a wonderful place to find out information.

Leaning against the bar, a glass of blood in my hand, I examine the crowd for any familiar faces. None stand out right away. Suddenly, my surveillance is interrupted by a large chest clad in a crisp white shirt. My eyes slowly scan upward to find two hazel eyes staring down at me. Immediately, I know what he is, and by the look in his eyes, what he wants.

"Hey darlin'. You here alone?"

"Yes. I assume you are with that group who can't stop watching us."

"They are part of my pack."

"I see."

"Do you want to head to the back?"

"Sorry, stud. I am here on business tonight."

"Come on. Don't be like that. You should be friendly."

"I am friendly. I'm so into sharing that if you don't leave me alone, I'm going to share your Lycan ass with the floor. Now, as I said, not tonight. Why don't you go learn how to treat others and then maybe we can talk sometime."

My eyes were glowing. I could tell from the way those around me backed up, and how clear my vision became. I saw through him. Not actually a bad guy, simply one acting the part in front of his friends. Definitely not the alpha of the pack. Lycans differed from werewolves. They had their mates, but they had much more freedom in choosing. In the end, they almost always ended up with their own kind to keep the bloodline pure.

I should have retained more control, but I was weary of

games. There were too many in progress lately. White eyes were not common, unless you were of a coven in the middle of some spell. Even then, they didn't radiate light.

A large hand landed on my shoulder. My gaze cut to see who it was as I heard the Lycan scurry off to his group. White eyes, white hair pulled back to reveal a tattoo down his neck that I didn't recognize.

"Come with me." He started to walk toward the back.

I followed, gulping down the remainder of my drink. We walked past the multiple rooms that could be secured for an hour, night, or even a few days. At the end of the hall was apparently his office. A beast of a man stood by the doorway, closing the door behind us with a nod toward his boss.

"We have never been properly introduced. My name is Alexander McKenzie. I am the Grand Coven Leader for the Americas and all connecting lands."

"A pleasure I'm sure, Mr. McKenzie. Tell me, why did you say 'No' when you saw me?"

"Because you shouldn't exist."

"Why not?"

"There is only supposed to be one Angel of Death. One that wields that power for when it is needed. It's not just that. The first time I saw you when I made the ring, I could sense the strength in your blood. When I saw you at The Agora, I could sense a deep dark magical imprint on you."

"Probably has something to do with my rebirth, thanks to Death. I want to know everything you might be able to tell me, but unfortunately, it has to wait. I am looking into who is behind a lot of disappearances lately. Do you know anything about that?"

"I do. Not who is behind it, but I know some exiled witches are using some of those taken to conduct spells that are forbidden. There are rumors that someone is trying to mess with the natural order. I thought most of it was nonsense, but then, I saw you."

"Seems to be the story of my life. Look, Alex, I am not trying to mess with your business or anything. I know others here might know more."

He stepped closer, towering over me, but his proximity didn't feel threatening. He raised his hand to tuck a strand of my hair behind my ear, all the while his eyes roamed over my face.

"I know, Jenna. I am also looking into this matter because of the coven. We can work together on this. While we do, I can assist you with figuring out why you were summoned. I do enjoy a good challenge."

"Then I suppose that is one thing we have in common. What I don't appreciate is others trying to toy with me. I believe you want to find out what's going on as much as I do. I'm not saying I trust you, but we can solve this faster if we aren't getting in each other's way."

"Your business here tonight is concluded then." He moved away to pick up a paper from his desk. Handing it to me, he held tight to his end while he spoke.

"This is the address we got off one of our regulars. I haven't had a chance to verify it yet, but I offer it to you as a sign of my cooperation."

"Thank you. I'll go check it out tonight."

"In that?"

I glanced down at my short red dress with knee high black boots and matching black jacket. The best disguises often didn't look like one. I arched a brow at Alex with a smile.

"Would you find me threatening if you saw me walking up like this?"

"In every possible way."

"Cute. I'll be fine and I will let you know what I find. You can get my number from Joanna."

"I would tell you to be careful, but I believe it isn't you that I have to worry about."

Outside the warehouse, I stood on a nearby rooftop watching for any signs of what was going on. About ten black vans pulled in through a sliding door. They were panel style, without windows along the back, and had serious 'down by the river' vibes. Every single one was driven by a shifter, vampire, or witch.

This was definitely the place. I ran along the roof, then leapt over to the building. Internally, a plea chimed on repeat. I pushed down on the internal monologue to focus on my goal. Climbing down a fire escape, I broke a window to crawl inside.

Creeping through the hallway, I found the main area lined with vans. A quick scan counted thirty people pushing or carrying others into cells against the back wall. From there, their view of the rest of the warehouse was obstructed. I watched longer, biding my time until I was certain I could tell who was in charge. If nothing else, that was the one I needed.

Making my way down unnoticed, the lights cut off. I didn't stop to think of my good fortune. I stepped from behind a large crate, hands on each side of a female shifter's head, and twisted.

The crack was muffled by the confused shouts from the others about the sudden darkness. Other voices near the other side of the warehouse rang out in alarm. A couple of shots fired in that direction made me pause a moment and look down at the dead female.

I didn't try to hide her body. I moved to my left, where I had seen three men talking. They were trying to raise others on a radio when I dashed forward. Elongated nails slashed through their necks in seconds, denying them the chance to cry out. Some of their blood sprayed my face, causing me to lick my lips. The taste made me wish I could have indulged.

Stealthily, I moved around the vans, growing bolder with each body that fell. A bullet tore through my shoulder and spun me around. Near the rear of the van was a vampire holding a Glock. My hand pressed against my shoulder, I started to move toward him, but he suddenly collapsed to the floor.

The lights, shots, now this. I was not alone. I decided to hurry to get the leader so I could question him about who was behind all this. Ascending the stairs to where I had seen them go, I halted in place. At the top of the stairs were both men, unconscious on the ground, with Alex standing over them.

"I decided I couldn't let you have all the fun. I was going to step in sooner, but you had all the others under control. Did you happen to leave any alive?"

"No. I planned to use the ones up here, so they weren't necessary."

"You really can switch your conscience on and off as it suits you."

"They were using people that didn't deserve it. I will not feel bad if they pay for it."

"It wasn't a jab, but a compliment. I feel the same way. I have men already set to clean this up. Once they remove everyone else, they will alert the police so they can come collect the mortals."

"You sound like you have done this a time or two."

"You aren't the only one who wants to keep the peace between our worlds. I don't care for mortals one bit. Doesn't mean I want to see them slaughtered."

"Fair enough. So what do we do about the ones we want to question?"

"I have an area we can go to where no one will hear them and they can't escape. I have more in the front of the warehouse to take with us as well."

"Sounds perfect."

was also at play here, but the combination could not go unnoticed.

In the open area, our guests waited. Alex was at a bench mixing some kind of concoction that I didn't ask questions about. The closest area to sit was on the edge of his bed. This, surprisingly seemed to have missed the overhaul. The mattress was firm, but it was covered in animal skins.

"You know, they make blankets that are quite warm."

"I prefer skin to skin."

He didn't turn around, and I was thankful for that when the sudden image of him naked beneath the pelts flashed behind my eyes. I had enough problems without complicating matters further.

"Ok, we are all set. Now, this may hurt a bit. Honestly, this will likely hurt a lot."

He went one by one and blew the dust into each of their faces. Some tried to hold their breath, but the cloud remained around them until they inhaled. Each coughed, doubling over as groans of pain echoed off the walls. When they were in a silent heap on the floor, he motioned for me to join him.

"They are all yours. They won't be able to lie. Even a half-truth will cause them excruciating pain until they reveal the truth."

"That's a nifty trick. A vial of that could come in handy."

"It won't work on him. He's seen too much pain as Death."

"Good to know." I turned my attention to the eight people currently trying to drag themselves into a seated position.

"Let me see if I have this right. We have two witches, three werewolves, and three vampires. Should we take bets on who cracks first? I really have only one question I care about. Who is behind this operation?"

Alex stood beside me, both of us watching as they shifted in their spots. The pain caused the vampires and the wolves to change. Claws and nails came out. Eyes morphed into red or yellow. Fangs grew within their mouths. The witches chanted, hoping to counter the spell. Their broken words evidence it wasn't working. At last, one of the werewolves screamed.

"Azrael. It's Azrael." They all yelled in unison.

"Why? Why would he do this?"

"Do you know who that is, Alex?"

"He's my brother."

They didn't wait this time for the pain to grow. The witch sobbed and began speaking quietly.

"Someone is killing them, Alex. He saw it. Two will die, one will live. He has been trying to stop it. He's been keeping them cloaked so no one could find them. Only now, since we didn't deliver." Her sobs grew louder.

"Who would want to kill the Fates? There wasn't much on them in Marcus' library."

"That will have to wait. Jenna, I'm sorry, but he's my brother."

That was the last thing I remember before a cloud of white dust flew in my face.

Wetness. Cold water dripping. A stream. The sun. Birds singing in a nearby tree. A shadow looming overhead as I try to look up at the sky from where I lay on the ground.

"Jenna? Jenna? I think she's coming around."

"Joanna." My head hurt, every noise rattled around and moving made me feel nauseous. "This must be what a hangover feels like."

"There is no time for jokes."

"Who's joking? Now where the fuck is Alex?"

"We don't know. He sealed off the entrance to his cave and his other residence. What happened? We found you in the hall unconscious."

"His brother is behind all the disappearances. I think he went to see him on his own, and whammied me so I couldn't stop him. They said that he was trying to stop the Fates from being killed. Two will die, one will live."

"Why wouldn't he come to us if he had a vision like that? We could have worked together to understand it and stop it."

"Arrogance and pride. Help me out here. Why is it so important that he would take to killing innocent people?"

"The Fates are not the end all of life, but they play a large part in destiny and free will. They can even manipulate the threads that bind us all if they are guided to do so. With two dead, the third will be bombarded by the guidance of all three. They could go mad, begin messing with our destiny, or begin cutting the threads short. There is also the possibility that whomever had the other two killed could keep the third and use them to do what they want until the other two are reincarnated."

"So essentially, the Fates are puppeteers and someone else wants to hold the strings. Got it. Point me in their direction and I will go deal with it."

"We can't. They are somewhere that none of our doors can go."

"Then how the hell is anyone supposed to kill them? This makes no sense."

"Azrael was likely using blood magic to reinforce their sanctuary. Taking mortal souls and using them to build a barrier essentially. Unfortunately, I actually think we may be too late."

CHAPTER 37
~ ADEMIA ~

I knew following those sniveling little weasels would work. They had been trying to get this done for the last seventy years. At the beginning there were six of them, now there were only four. Two had died during their last attempt. I may or may not have had a hand in it.

This was a source of amusement for me. Torture got boring after a while, and there had not been any special tasks for about ten years. At least none they gave me to complete. The leash seemed to be getting tighter and tighter. If things continued, I would be confined to my room before long. That would be true torture.

"Do you have it?"

"Yes, the witch told me where to find it, so I would stop."

"Then let's go. We will show them all what we can do. Maybe he will reward us."

One of them pulled out a golden amulet I couldn't make out clearly. He tossed it on the ground and immediately a tear opened above it. I watched them all congratulate each other, then slip one by one through the opening.

"Sorry boys." I followed behind them.

Stepping through, a small cottage waited in front of me. Screams could be heard through the shattered door. These idiots may end up killing them all. The idea made me smile. I wonder how the chaos of their deaths would impact everything else.

I needed the last of them to bargain for whatever it was he thought I had done. It was the only explanation for why I was suddenly on lock down. I tried to think of where I messed up, but every assignment given had been done with precision. So what was it?

Moving forward, I caught a flash of red in a bush to the right. My eyes rolled as I walked straight over and shoved my hand between the branches to drag her out. Long red hair wrapped around my fist, tears were streaming down her face, and golden eyes met mine.

"They killed them. They killed my sisters."

"Lucky for you they did, or you would be the one to die."

The four idiots came out when they heard her scream from being dragged toward the tear. I heard them begin running, so I punched her in the back of her skull to keep her compliant. She dropped to the ground in time for me to dodge the first blow.

I didn't waste my time fighting them. They were among our lowest ranks and would not be missed by anyone. A snap of my fingers was all it took. Where four demons had stood, four piles of ash remained. I watched the wind scatter them as I bent down and grabbed one of her arms. I lifted her easily up and over my shoulder.

I needed to keep her away while I negotiated, which meant only one thing. A trip to go see Goldilocks. I despised dealing with the goodie two shoes every time, but this time it was a necessity. I paused by the tear, the golden amulet was the only thing to exist on both sides.

Giving it a chance, I spoke clearly while considering killing her if this didn't work. Only it did. The Agora hallway formed around me as I stepped through. I didn't move. I knew it wouldn't take long for her to come with her superiority complex to ask me why I was here.

"What are you doing here, and who is that woman? Quickly, someone get her to the clinic."

"Try to take her from me and I will find a way to end you. I need to talk to Goldilocks."

"That is not her name."

"Like I give a shit. Take me to her. Now."

Sitting in the office, I was still trying to get my bearings while we all tried to think of a solution. Many of the passages used would not work. The ones that might, would require knowing the precise location of the Fates.

"We have to save them, or all those people died for nothing. Alex had better deal with his brother before I do." I raised my brow at Joanna.

"Jenna, one problem at a time. We need to get them and bring them here." She replied.

"They control fate. Can't they see what is going on?" Carissa chimed in.

"Not if it directly involves them. This way, they cannot alter someone else's destiny in favor of their own." Joanna confirmed.

"We have to face facts. They are going to die. We can't get to them and we don't know who wants them dead. So what do we do once they are dead? Will anyone be able to tell? Can we track whatever one lives and bring her here?" I stood and began to pace.

"I'm afraid Jenna is right, dear. We have to start preparing." Joanna looked at her daughter with concern in her eyes.

In the silence, they shared one of those infuriating looks. Again, something was going on and I was in the dark.

"Seems we don't have to wait, or search." Joanna broke the silence as she turned toward the door just as it opened.

A tall, thin woman carrying a redhead over her shoulder strolled in casually. She hoisted the sleeping woman into a chair, then sat on the desk with her boot on the armrest.

She was wearing torn up jeans, two tank tops, both of which were loose and low cut to reveal the multiple tattoos on her arms, chest, back and stomach.

"I claim sanctuary." She said, while lighting a cigarette with her finger.

"What?" They both responded in unison.

"Someone want to fill me in? Who the hell are they?" I took a step forward.

Joanna had moved to examine the redhead, an audible gasp resounding when she looked into her eyes.

"You did it. You killed them." Carissa's voice raised in alarm.

"Sorry, but that honor wasn't mine. I got there too late, but just in time to nab that one." The stranger smirked.

"Then we're good. We have the Fate and can just keep her safe." I sighed in relief.

"It's not that simple, Jenna." Carissa shook her head.

"What do you mean, Carissa? Who is this woman?" I put my hand on the dagger I kept at my hip.

"She's claimed sanctuary. As long as she isn't harming the Fate, we can't intervene." Carissa folded her arms.

"You can't. Doesn't mean I can't." I slipped the blade free only to feel my body freeze under the effects of The Agora.

"Actually, it does, sweet cheeks. That's the law of this place. Something they have tried to get changed, but until it is... Anyone that tries to interfere or take what's mine will be exiled."

"What the fuck? You guys can't be serious."

"Unfortunately, we are. If you do anything, we will have no choice but to banish you." Joanna confirmed.

The woman sat, letting the smoke she inhaled escape slowly with inky black eyes. How I hated demons.

"Don't worry, hotness. I am not going to let anything happen to my little trinket. Unless she asks nicely."

"That's enough, Ademia. You've made your point. A room will be made available to you. I am assuming you will not be remaining the entire time, but you know that even when you are not here, your guest will not be taken away from here." Joanna bit out.

"I knew I could count on you two."

She hefted the woman over her shoulder once more with a smile.

"I am sure I'll be seeing you around. Jenna, right?"

"Yes, and you're Ademia. If you're the one I've heard about. You're also known as Lucifer's Fire."

"Awe, you have heard of me. Don't worry, I won't kill everyone, no matter what the voices in my head say." She laughed, her dark brown hair falling over her shoulder when she turned to leave.

Once she was gone, I saw the others visibly relax. Joanna startling me when she went to the cabinet to pour herself a drink. Carissa opened her mouth to say something, then clenched her jaw and left the room quickly.

"Jenna, I hate to ask this, but we would appreciate if you remained on the grounds. The situation is far more dire than we anticipated. If she has the Fate, there is only one person she will want to hand her over to."

"Lucifer." I confirmed.

"If he gets his hands on the last remaining Fate, I shudder to think of the consequences."

"Then we just won't let that happen. Is there some law or

loophole that would allow us to free her?"

"We will have to confirm. The laws were set up with all the reigning families. If we were to break them, we would lose their trust and, with it, the peace we have enjoyed."

CHAPTER 39
~ JENNA ~

Exhausted, I agreed to stay on site. They set me up in a room down the hall from Ademia and her captive. Laying on top of the bed, I tried to recall everything I had heard of her. Only my aching head refused to cooperate.

I owed Alex for this lesson in misery. A debt I looked forward to repaying. I just had to hope his brother hadn't decided to kill him like he did all those innocent people. Granted, some did some very illegal things but, other than the traffickers, they deserved judgment and not whatever torture they endured.

I can imagine the fight between the two of them, if Azrael is anything like Alex. I learned after he had forged the ring how powerful Alex is. He was born with a natural ability to use magic. As I've come to learn about all witches, magic is all around us and many could tap into it if they practiced. The more powerful mages, warlocks, and witches were born connected to the flow that resides in all things.

I was a little disappointed to have missed the battle. More so, I wonder how I would have done if I fought both at once. Two of the most powerful beings in their community, against me. The outcast. No surprise now why the elders always despised me. Being a halfling wasn't bad enough. I was stronger, and no one knew why.

That's going to be another issue to face. What will they have to say when they find out I am a part of Death? I know only one thing for certain: I will be summoned once they hear the news. Brought before them, not because they will accept me, but as a show of power that I yield to their authority.

What has that humility gotten me? Nothing. The rare times I saw one of them, I was basically ignored. Which was fine. They didn't know me and I am not some high-ranking person in their society. What twisted my nipples was when they would ask a question directed at me to someone else. Marcus had stood there playing telephone for an hour once when we were at a meeting they called for all our kind in the territory. Our kind. Can I even say that?

Frustrated, I left to head to the gym. Here, the equipment was much different from a mortal one. There were rooms for practicing spells, fire, ice, water, earth, weaponry of all types, and workout machines and free weights. The machines varied in sizes and weight limits.

I stretched, then headed up a set of stairs to run on the track that was against the wall. Running for an hour did nothing to ease my nerves. Chest press, bicep curls, leg abduction, machine after machine I pushed to the maximum weight I could handle. Sweat didn't begin to bead along my forehead until I had passed six hours.

Giving up, I knew nothing was going to alleviate the rawness I felt. Heading back to my room, I didn't make it down the hall before Carissa came running up to me. She was out of breath, panting, while she formed the words.

"We...we found it. The loophole. There is a way."

"Perfect. Let's do it then."

"You don't understand. It's a fight. A fight to the death. Winner takes what the other has and their life."

"What? What kind of barbaric bullshit is this?"

She shot me a look that I mimicked back to her.

"This is extreme to keep people from doing it, Jenna."

"Well, we can't let Ademia hand off the Fate to Lucifer. How do we do this? Knowing you guys, it's some formal process."

"You have to challenge her, and state what you want if you win. Then, she must accept your challenge. After that, we will send you both with the prize into an arena where you will have full use of any special skills."

"Ok."

"Ok?"

"Yeah, ok. She's a demon. I think we will be fine with one less around. Besides, I might as well live up to my reputation."

CHAPTER 40
~ ADEMIA ~

I poked her with the knife I was using to carve into the walls. A small trickle of blood ran down her shoulder. She'd been asleep for a few hours, and I was getting bored.

"Wake the fuck up already. For Lucifer's sake, damn."

"Huh? Where am I? Oh no, the demons. My sisters. Where are they?" She shot straight up in the bed, looking around like she was going to run home.

"They're dead. All of them. Demons too."

"You saved me. Why did you save me?"

"I need you. Plain and simple. You are my get out of jail free card because I pissed the man off. I'll go talk to him later tonight and then tomorrow, you'll get a warm introduction yourself."

"I need to go home. I can't be here. They'll come back, and I need to be there when they do."

"What's your name? They had to call you something."

"Vanessa. Vanessa Canders."

"K, I'm Ademia. You're not going home. It ain't safe. You're just gonna chill here for a bit. Then you'll come home with me. Got it?"

"I appreciate you saving me and looking out for me, but I really must go home. When they return, they will wonder where I am. They will have questions."

"You aren't listening. You are not going home. Not now. Not ever again. So, get used to it."

Vanessa began to sob into her hands, her knees brought up to her chest. Fucking pathetic. Tempted to slap her, a knock on the door interrupted the moment. The flames in my eyes ignited over the disruption, my hand nearly tearing the knob out of the door when I opened it to find them standing there.

"What do you want?"

"Such a cordial welcome. I don't understand how so many could be unhappy in Hell."

"What do you and Goldilocks here want? I'm a little busy."

"That's why we're here. I formally challenge you to a fight to the death, for your prisoner, the Fate."

"You want to fight me for her? Are you nuts? You don't stand the chance."

"Does that mean you accept her challenge? I need an official yes or no for our records." Goldilocks spoke up.

"No. I don't have time for her."

"Carissa, let the record show that the demon chose not to fight. Make sure to send a copy to her Master."

"What the fuck did you just say?" Lucifer had one lesson he gave often. Always fight, always win. I knew Goldilocks would do it, too. Sending him that note when I was trying to negotiate with him would not help me.

"You know what? Fine. We can have our little challenge. Your head on a pike will make a nice addition to his tribute."

"Ok, tomorrow afternoon you will face each other for the possession of the Fate."

"Vanessa." I corrected out of spite.

"What?"

"Her name."

"Oh, ok. I'll make note of it."

The words were barely out when I slammed the door in their faces. So, the newbie wanted a fight. I wasn't concerned. Killing her would mean a small offering before I brought the Fate to him. This actually couldn't have worked out any better.

~ JENNA ~

I sat with Carissa and Joanna, talking about the challenge. Joanna's concern was still so motherly. It almost warmed my heart. Who was I kidding? Nothing ever made a great impact on me. It hadn't for years.

Getting ready to face Ademia, I was ready to die if need be. Excusing myself, I went to the bathroom. The bourbon I consumed, to the dismay of Joanna, was requesting release. Admittedly, I was thankful for the distraction. Their melancholy expressions were wearing thin.

Washing my hands, I caught sight of the mirror waving like the top of a clear lake kissed by the wind. I turned off the water, shaking my hands as I took a step back. From the reflective surface, he came walking through. A long black jacket over a black shirt, jeans, and shoes. I crossed my arms while looking him over.

"You do know they make doors and other colors exist, right?"

"I heard about your fight. You can't take this lightly."

He kept advancing until my back was pressed to the wall behind me. Our breath mingled, and I realized my heart was suddenly racing.

"Why are you doing this to me?"

"Talking sense into you or how you want me as much as I want you? The second part isn't anything I am doing to you, anymore than you are doing it to me."

"They say it's not a good idea to fuck before a competition."

"You need to keep your mind on the fight, not your libido."

"Then shut up already."

I grabbed the back of his head, my lips crashing against his. Any argument he had died as he lifted me to set me on the counter. Hands fumbled between our bodies to undo our pants and push them down. As soon as the cool air touched my skin, he grabbed both my wrists and held them behind me.

My ass on the edge, he used his other hand to position himself and drive into my core. The muscles wrapped tightly around him, his hands shifting to hold my hips in place. I locked my ankles, pulling my hands free to grip his shoulders. He leaned down, our mouths muffling the groans that echoed off the tile walls. He felt good. I smiled into our kiss with amusement at the thought swirling around my mind.

Raw need carried us on. His hips plunging him deep within my body over and over again. The sound of each thrust lost to the rising moans that fell from my lips. Within minutes, he had me on the edge and sent me over without hesitation. His body slowing with the last remnants of his own orgasm subsiding.

We stood there without moving. Forehead to forehead with random kisses that threatened to reignite the inferno. He seemed reluctant to pull away, and until he did, I didn't realize I hadn't wanted him to either.

"I'm sorry. I didn't mean to do that." The sincerity in his voice made me free a small laugh.

"Could have fooled me. Wonder what you're like when you actually mean to fuck someone senseless."

"One day, I'll show you."

With a smirk, he leaned in to leave a long lingering kiss to my lips, then vanish.

I pulled up my pants to stand on legs that surprisingly trembled. Facing the mirror, I smiled and did my best to smooth away the evidence that my world had just been turned upside down. Exiting the bathroom, I stopped when I found them both waiting there.

Joanna and Carissa looked me over with raised brows, causing me to shrug.

"Let's just say, 'Fuck Death' has a whole new meaning."

Carissa burst out laughing. Joanna seemed to need a moment to catch on to my meaning. Her cheeks burned bright red as she cleared her throat and headed to the door.

"Well, I hope you're ready then. It's time."

CHAPTER 42
~ ADEMIA ~

Vanessa and I headed down to the arena that was set up. We entered to see everyone else standing in the center. To the left was a small box seat with a bench. I directed Vanessa to it with my hand on the woman's arm before she could really see anyone.

"So, you don't get any ideas about playing with the threads."

I wrapped a black cloth over her eyes, waving my hand and causing a few sparks to make sure she couldn't see. All threads may have passed through her home, but they were all around us. Last thing I needed was her playing with one to affect the outcome of this fight.

"You ready, Ademia?"

"You that eager to die?"

"If that is supposed to be intimidating, you might want to try again."

"Ok, both of you. This fight is hereby permitted. The winner will be awarded with the Fate and the life of the other. This is the last chance for either party to back out. When we reach our viewing station, all doors will disappear until the battle is over."

I watched Jenna stretch and glance around the arena. She seemed calculating, which in my experience meant she would end up being predictable, once I learned her style.

I wanted to enjoy the battle. I stood waiting for her to make her first move. She circled as if she was sizing me up, but it was her feet that gave her away. She had studied martial arts. The soft steps, the way her feet were placed to react to any attack. I had heard she was skilled; I knew the rumors about her circled even the depths of Hell. No one knew though, exactly what she was.

There was a presence that radiated off her. An energy that said she had strength. It had been too long since I felt I had a real challenge. I wanted to draw this out for as long as I could. The unfortunate part was that my patience was thin. Having a little fun with her, I made the ground at her feet heat till the stones became red.

She jumped back, a curse spilling from her lips. I used the chance to lunge forward, tackling her to the ground. I felt nails slice through my shirt. Her fangs nipped at my neck in an attempt to tear into the vein. I laughed. The pain, the struggle, the adrenaline all amused me.

"You can do better than that." I screamed as I brought flames up to circle around us.

Tossing her back, her arm broke the barrier to singe her flesh. The sizzling sound was music to my ears. My eyes went black to match my nails, my skin growing leathery as wings rolled from my back. My true demonic form on full display felt wonderful.

Jenna stood, raising her arm to show how the burn was nothing more than a pink mark that was already fading away. This was going to be fun. Vampires always heal from most wounds, but not that fast. Seeing the wound vanish so quickly only served to make me want to test her limits.

With a gust of wind, I rose above her to descend quickly and steal a chunk from her shoulder. I heard her cry out, her other hand immediately covering the gash as she dropped to her knees and shot a look up.

"Bitch."

"Yes?"

She surprised me when she ran through the flames to the wall lined with weapons. A spear with a long silver tip was thrown before I knew which she would choose. It hit the mark, cutting through my wing to embed itself high in the wall behind me. I landed hard on the soil, the wind kicked from my lungs. Now this was a fight. I jumped to my feet only to have to duck as Jenna swung a longsword, narrowly missing my head.

I kicked out, landing my heel in the middle of her abdomen, then punched her in the jaw before she could rise. Blood sprayed from her lips, a dark bruise forming instantly. Going for a jab, she caught my fist in her hand.

The sound of bones crunching under the force of her grip accompanied the crackle of the flames dancing nearby. I grit my teeth, my smile growing wider until I burst out laughing.

"Damn, this is fun!"

"That the best you got? I thought demons were tougher."

"Let's see you heal from this, bitch."

Flames engulfed us, swirling around like a tornado that rose from the floor to the ceiling. The tight cyclone made the ground rise in waves around our feet. Jenna's cry was short, too short. Dismayed, I walked from the inferno to watch her shadowy form drop.

"You can bring back the doors. It's over."

"The doors open when the other is dead."

On hearing their words, I turned back to the dying flames to see her crouched down on the ground. Her clothing was gone, destroyed in the fire. Her skin resembling crisp bacon left too long in the pan. But what made me clap, was her starting to stand.

If the way she moved was any indication, she was in pain. As she stepped toward me, the burnt flesh dropped in pieces. Shedding to reveal pristine skin beneath. No vampire I had ever known could heal quickly enough to survive something that hot. Even if they had, to walk away already whole was unimaginable.

CHAPTER 43

~ JENNA ~

I was numb. All I could see were the flames devouring my body, then nothing. I dropped with the knowledge that I would die, but then I felt nothing. There was nothing. No sound. No fire. No pain. No heat. I stayed like that, wondering if this was what death felt like. So peaceful.

As I rose and approached Ademia, I began to feel again. The soil beneath my feet, the wind on my skin. The sound of her clapping. I stopped when we were practically touching. We stood staring at one another until my hand shot out and grabbed her by the throat.

I lifted her up off the ground. The ground that I noticed seemed so far away. My eyes were glowing white with swirls of black. I knew it because I could see the way the colors changed my vision and revealed her to me. This was new. Stronger than it ever had been before.

"Do you surrender?"

"You have to kill me."

"No, I don't. The law says I get your life. That means it is mine to choose what to do with. So, I ask again. Do you surrender?"

"Fuck you."

"I'm going to take that as a yes."

I dropped her. The thud from her landing telling me she had earned a few more broken bones. Landing. I realized then that I was flying. Death's words came rushing back to me, but I couldn't bring myself to believe that this demon was the one who was supposed to know me and tell me who I really am.

Instinctively, I came back down to a cursing demon and a silenced Joanna and Carissa. They reached out to touch my wings, which were white. They were not black or even grey, but a pure white. Hearing a commotion behind me, I remembered what this fight was about.

The redhead came rushing forward, crying. She wrapped her arms around me tight, mumbling something I couldn't hear through her sobs. Joanna placed a robe around me, my wings disappearing as she did. I pushed Vanessa back to tie it at my waist.

She stood smiling at me, staring as if she had just found a puppy. She looked so innocent that I just wanted to protect her. Keep her this way, untarnished by the world. Unable to control herself, she lunged forward to embrace me again. This time her head by my ear.

"Oh, my goodness. I never thought you would be here. We didn't know what happened. You had just left. Dead and then just poof. But you're back. You're really back."

"Slow down. Do you know who I am? I mean was?"

"Yes, absolutely. Your thread has always been unique. It's different now, but I knew at once that it was you. My sisters and I always missed you. You were always so kind."

"Now I really think you have her confused with someone else." Carissa interjected.

"Shut up." Turning back to Vanessa, I grabbed both of her shoulders. "Tell me. Tell me who I was before I was reborn."

"You don't know? You should know."
"Just tell me. We can get into the rest later. Who am I?"
"Why, you're Eve."

~ To be continued... ~

THE STORY OF SALAZAR AND EVE

The day was glorious. The sun shone down over the fields behind the home they shared. She lay there in their bed sound asleep. The twilight hours had found them wrapped within each other's arms until exhaustion demanded she rest. He could not. Sleep had not been a necessity for him for ages. Instead, he snuck off to plant a cherry tree in the clearing where they had sat during the day. Surrounded by the forest, the patch of soft green earth had been their sanctuary. She had teased that the only thing missing was a single solitary tree with something they could indulge in.

Eve was the only woman he had ever met that accepted him for what he was. He had existed long before humans began to evolve. He fed on the animals around him until the day he tasted the sweet elixir held in their veins. How the crimson flow sustained him far better than anything else did not give him pause. He considered them to be another animal to satisfy his appetite. It all changed when they began to speak, to innovate, to become more familiar. Even then he feasted on hem without remorse.

Eve was different. Smiling at how the sun filtered through the window to warm the brown tones of her long hair, he surrendered to the memory of their first encounter.

The moon rose high in the sky, lending its glow to the forest below. The shadows stretched out, bare wooden fingers searching for some unknown treasure. She knelt by the river, jug in her hands to capture the cool water. He hungered for her blood, her scent floating on the wind urging him to come closer.

He struck as she stood. The heavy clay crashing on the rocks along the water's edge. She cried out startling the animals of the night. Her fear made her blood more enticing. However when he pulled back to relish in his meal, her eyes locked on his own to banish any other thought. All at once, he wanted to protect this fragile creature. She needed to be his and his alone. A switch flipped that he never knew existed. There was not fear in her gaze, or even defeat, she held strength, anger, and hope. Even as her life was being drained, she refused to give in.

He licked her neck, effectively slowing the flow of blood as he held her hair in his hand. Refusing to remove his eyes until the wound closed to leave two pink scars. Never had he tried to stop the flowing drink. His amazement to see it work curled his lips to one side.

"Are you going to kill me?" The feminine voice brought his eyes back to hers.

"No. I don't think I would like you to die."

"Then what are you going to do with me?"

"I'm not sure. I think I would like to keep you."

"Saints willing, sir. I will see you dead before I am your slave." She kicked him hard between the legs, the surprise causing him to loosen his grip enough for her to take off back toward the town.

His laughter erupted from his chest without warning.

The following night he waited in the nearby woods for her to appear. Minutes passed into hours, night into day but she never came. The next night held more of the same, and the next, and the next. Five nights passed before he saw her again. He waited until she was crouched by the water then stepped out onto the path. Making sure his steps crunched on the loose pebbles, he held his hands up when her head turned to find him.

"Please wait." His tone was even.

"Did you come to bite me again?" Her voice was steady despite the quickening of her pulse.

"No. I've already fed."

"Then why have you come?"

"I needed to see you. You intrigue me."

"The Gods have certainly blessed me then." She turned back to pick up the large pot, uncaring that he stood only a couple feet away.

Puzzled, he could only study her until he realized that she did not mean what she had said. At least not in a straight forward sense. Moving toward her, he went to take the heavy water filled pot from her hands but she did not relinquish it right away. Instead, they stood with their fingers touching, eyes locked in a mix of challenge and contemplation.

Cautiously her hands fell to her sides, a deep sigh causing her chest to rise and fall. In silence they walked back to her home. He set the pot down on the table where she pointed, then waited uncertain what to do for the first time in his existence. After several minutes, he left.

For weeks, they completed this same ritual until he was meeting her at her door and walking with her to the water then back again. He was beginning to wonder if he would ever hear her speak to him. He even found himself yearning for a single word.

Then one night when he was preparing to go, she cleared her throat. Abruptly he turned to face her and found her pointing to a seat by the table.

"Would you like to stay for a while?"

"Yes."

"Will you tell me what you are?" She sat across from him.

"I am not sure what I am. Humans have taken to calling those similar to me, vampires or monsters."

"Are you not a vampire?"

"Those I have seen do not have wings like I do."

She nearly choked on the water she swallowed, the question coming out on a forced exhale, "Wings?"

He rose, taking a couple steps back to the only open area within the modest dwelling and unfurled wings black as night. The candlelight caught along the feathers giving off blue and purplish hues. Her mouth hung open, her breaths coming harder as her heart beat erratically within the confined space.

"Beautiful." She whispered.

They began to visit each other more often. Her first attempts to find him lending him some amusement. He had long ago set up residence within a nearby cave. What was to be a temporary location had become his home as he stayed to be near her.

Countless hours were more precious to him than eons passed. He answered all of her questions and she required he assist her in her chores. He discovered she was skilled with repairing most anything brought to her. From a wheel to a table to a dress or a pot. He began to look forward to every moment with her and yet he longed for more.

One day, they were clearing traps in the river when he slipped on a stone and fell in. The bellowing laughter from the shore quickly faded as he reached to pull her in to him. One splash was all she was permitted, his lips found hers, a moment of hesitation melting to draw her hands behind his neck.

There, waist deep in the river, he sated the desire he couldn't deny. Buried within her body, something inside his own shattered. With every thrust of his hips, her voice cried out his name. He tore the top of her dress to expose more of her flesh to his gaze. His mouth hungered to taste the supple skin that pebbled under his tongue. Harder he drove into her, the water around their bodies a chaotic symphony of small waves. Falling over the edge as one, instinct brought his fangs into her vein and one thought to mind: *MINE*

Coming down from the heat of the moment, he opened his mouth to apologize only to have her lift up to steal his words with a kiss that spoke volumes. From that moment on, he was with her always. He felt that all was right within the world.

That was until he showed up. Six months later, a man appeared in town. Salazar learned his name was Adam. A son of a long standing family, returned from some voyage that was to bring him wealth. He had been moderately successful in his endeavor, yet a smile was not on display when they went to greet him.

By day's end, Salazar discovered how Adam coveted Eve. Her assurances that the feelings were not reciprocated soothed the protective nature in danger of rising up. He has been a nuisance since but Eve continued to assure that he was nothing to concern themselves with.

She stirred, a soft groan escaping her parted lips. Slowly her eyes opened, a smile spreading across her face when she realized she had an audience. He still wondered how he went from the man she loathed to the man she swore to love with all her being.

"Hello, handsome."

"Hello, my missing piece."

"You know there are much easier titles you might call me." She laughed as she left the bed to sit on his lap.

"Perhaps, but I wish to speak the truth. I was not complete until I found you and I did not even know it."

He kissed her forehead, savoring how she softened into him. Her arms draped over his shoulders, her stomach alerting them to her need for food. With a slight pout, she removed herself to gather eggs and begin preparing a meal. He had learned to cook alongside her but it was a skill he had not mastered. Food was only tolerable to him in very small quantities. Blood is what he craved, hers especially if only to share all he could with her.

She had come to enjoy the small tastes he took from her as well. Of course, he did all he could so that he did not hurt her or take too much. In truth he didn't need much to remain vital. Lately, he felt like being with her is what gave him life. Even now, watching her cook her breakfast, he felt more alive than he ever had before she crossed his path.

As the day languished on, they made their way outdoors. Salazar lead Eve to the woods, then further till they reached the clearing. The surprise he had anticipated sharing lost to the swing of an axe. The tree he called upon to grow lay in pieces. The gleam of the axe resting where the trunk once stood. Next to the massacre, a tall muscular frame dripping sweat smirked their way.

"Adam." Eve stated tightly.

"My lovely Eve. I see you still care for this spot in the woods. I don't recall there being this annoying tree in the center before but I took care of it."

"A shame. I think the tree would have been a beautiful addition." She placed her hand on Salazar's chest knowingly.

"Salazar. I would have thought you would have moved on by now. Isn't that what your kind does?" Adam pulled the axe from the wood to rest against his shoulder.

"There aren't others like me, Adam. Though I appreciate your concern. I think I will be staying permanently though. I can't imagine a better place to spend my years."

"Eve, are you seriously going to allow him to stay with you? You deserve a life. A real life. He isn't human. He won't even age. I bet he can't even give you a family." Adam exploded.

"Adam, calm down. I love him and I will gladly take any time I can have with him."

"You will regret this. Both of you." Adam gritted his teeth and stormed off.

Eve looked up at Salazar, unease shining in her eyes. He wrapped her in his arms, curling her into his body hoping it made her feel safe.

"Come. We can enjoy the day still. The tree will regrow. I will see to it for you." Salazar placed a kiss to the top of her head and pulled her to the ground with him.

They sat in silence, the breeze lightly tossing their hair from their faces, birds chirping in the distance. If not for the stump and mangled branches a few feet away, they could fool themselves into thinking the day was nothing but pleasant.

"Eve?"

"Yes?"

"What was between you and Adam? He is far too angry for a rejected man."

She sighed with a slight tremble, her fingers interlocking with his before she turned to face him.

"Adam and I grew up together. He often said from the time we came of age that one day we would marry. For a time, I thought he was right. He was once so kind and gentle. He was known to help all those around without complaint. We spent a lot of time together."

A stray tear slipped from her right eye, his thumb brushing it away without a word. He could tell there was more and he did not wish to push her.

"As we became closer, he began to change. That or perhaps I was just learning who he truly was. If I was late, he questioned me for every minute. If I helped or spoke to another man, he sometimes started fights with them. He even took to sabotage the work of others then do the repairs himself to garner the affections of the others. I began to avoid him. Eventually I told him I could not be with him. He had slapped me in front of his family. The next day they sent him away. He had written me a note that he would return for me one day. No doubt his family told him that I was with another."

Her smile returned, however unsteady. He leaned in to press his lips to hers, wishing he could take her sadness into himself.

Over the next several months, whispers grew in number and voice. The crops mysteriously failed. The meeting house caught fire. Some of the livestock fell ill. Word was spreading that Salazar was to blame. The he was bringing curses to them all because they have allowed him to remain. Some took it upon themselves to warn Eve about the danger she was in. As she swore they were wrong, they feared she was under his control.

They both knew who had set their predicament in motion yet finding proof was not easy. While they hoped everything would settle, matters only became more dire. When half the livestock was found mutilated, no one would listen to reason.

The following morning, blood was splattered across their front door. A pig's head was on a their fence post the next day.

"Eve, we should leave this place. The two of us can go anywhere. I promise you that I will give you a life of peace, of happiness."

"Salazar, this has always been my home. I don't know if I can leave it."

She kissed his cheek, rolled from the bed to dress then grabbed the jug to head down to the river. The night before she had told him she wanted to go alone. His presence had set others off in recent days and she now more than ever wanted a day of ease to consider his offer.

"I will return soon. I will think about what you have said, my love."

"Please do, my missing piece." He returned the smile that brightened her face at his words.

When she had gone, he rose to straighten up and do something he rarely attempted. He set everything on the table and sat staring out the window for a while. He wanted to give her time so the food would be warm when she came home. An hour passed, he started making breakfast.

Cracking the eggs, he was careful not to break the yokes knowing how she enjoyed dipping the bread she made in the yellow liquid. It took a few tries and twice as many discarded eggs to get it right. Placing the food on the table, he became aware of the sun's position in the sky.

"Where are you?" He whispered to himself.

A sickening feeling took up residence in his chest. Internally he reminded himself that she wanted to think. What he was asking of her was not an easy decision to make and if he was honest with himself, he feared her choice if he pushed. He forced himself to wait another hour until he couldn't take it anymore.

Making his way to the water, he thought about when he first

met Eve. A smile spread across his lips until the scent of blood wafted in with the spring air. There was no mistaking that scent. Even as his brain registered what he was smelling, his legs propelled him forward.

Laying by the bank, Eve appeared as if she were sleeping. As he neared he noticed the red stain that spread over her dress into the earth beneath her. His knees gave way beside her body, his chest constricted. He scooped her up into his arms to hold her against him. Silent tears fell from his cheeks onto her head.

Night ruled the sky when an angry shout brought him back to present. He heard but did not respond to the voice that remained muffled to his ears. The world meant nothing to him. Everything could fade to nothing around him. There was an emptiness within him unlike anything he had ever felt before.

"NO!" Adam hit Salazar in the head with a large branch.

"This is your fault. If you hadn't bewitched her. If you hadn't..." Adam tried to take Eve's body from Salazar.

Blood dripped down the side of his face, he could feel that but he could not feel the pain of the wound. Getting to his feet, Salazar instantly let one emotion overshadow all others: Vengeance.

"Did you do this, Adam?"

"No. She was mine. She belonged to me."

"Did you do this?"

"The people are afraid of you. So they were afraid of her too. You are the cause of this. You killed her."

In an instant, Salazar had Adam by the throat. He wanted to snap his neck, to tear him limb from limb. The only thing that stopped him was the thought of Eve seeing him now.

"I will never forgive you or your kind. I will relish every death of your short, pathetic lives. You feared what you called the reaper of souls, but you will fear me more. Each of your deeds will be a stone to seal your fate. Your death will be special and one I will watch gladly."

"I won't give you the satisfaction. You're a monster and I won't forgive you for taking her from me."